PHOENIX REBORN

Sons of the Phoenix: Book 2

A novel by

JOSEPH MACKAY

To Connor and Alex
For whom there are no limits

PHOENIX REBORN

Sons of the Phoenix: Book 2

PROLOGUE

THE WORLD HAD CHANGED.

In 2051, mankind had drained the Earth of its fossil fuels. For years, humanity's best scientists looked for alternative forms of energy to help sustain life on Earth. Many technologies were created, but none could satisfy man's rate of consumption.

In 2074, a team of oceanic explorers uncovered the wreckage of an alien vessel at the bottom of the Pacific Ocean. Among the early discoveries made while studying the ship was slipstream technology. This discovery gave man the ability to increase particles faster than light, allowing the creation and stabilization of wormholes. It wasn't long after that humanity discovered a way to follow the particles through the folds in space time.

Probes were sent out at first and, soon after, manned exploratory flights, searching for habitable planets and other viable resources. In 2095, the first colony vessels were sent through slipstream folds to various star systems to establish livable conditions on habitable planets and report on the level of available resources. Most colonies performed their function as best they could with limited interaction with the United Earth Defense Force (UEDF), the collaboration of Earth's nations and governments.

Soon the majority of the population of Earth became complacent, satisfied to let the global government use these worlds to help sustain human life.

For nearly forty years, the Earth Military Council (EMC) of

the United Earth Defense Force studied the alien vessel to learn what other secrets it possessed. They raised it from the ocean floor through a feat of engineering and moved it to a secret location on the island of Kita-Daito, near Japan. However, none of their efforts allowed access to the inside of the ship, until they discovered the device.

They called it OMBI; the Omni-Manifold Bracer Implant, which, by connecting to the dominant arm of its host, allowed for the free exchange of binary data and human thought. The first tests resulted in a mental overload of information, causing the brain to shut down, killing the host. Inhibitor chips were designed and added to the OMBI, but the operators still suffered from brain malfunctions and ultimately ended up going insane after a few days of use.

It was by accident that a researcher discovered the device performed better when used by a child. Children, with their developing brains, had proven more successful in binding with the synapse-sync technologies; fusing their brain functions with operating computers allowed them to experience combat, piloting and operating functions with the speed of thought.

In need of viable hosts for the OMBI devices and sensing the unrest of the population of Earth, the Earth Military Council (EMC), under the leadership of General Harruhama, staged an attack on the colonies under the guise of an alien threat. The Gortha were invented by the EMC and blamed for the attack. They were characterized by Earth's media as an evil race of lizard-like humanoids with superior technology and a hunger for planetary resources. In 2115, in response to the Gortha threat, the UEDF was taken over by the EMC, putting General Harruhama in charge as a global dictator.

The people lived in fear of humanity's new enemy, getting sporadic media reports from the front lines of the battle, mankind's colonies.

Under the guise of needing better resources to battle the Gortha threat, the EMC opened the Ombicademy within the halls of the alien vessel. Children were drafted into military service for their ability to safely connect with the alien technology, in order to facilitate the unlocking of the ship's mysteries and technologies.

Humanity was all too willing to offer its brightest children to their government to protect the human race, all in the name of the greater good.

CHAPTER 1

Phoenix

"IT'S ONLY BEEN THREE MONTHS; WE NEED TO BE patient if we are going to have a chance at any of this," Major Edmond Sanders said into the communicator on his datapad, the dark figure on the screen nodding thoughtfully at Sander's report.

He had been recruiting and acting as an evaluation consultant for the Earth Military Council at the Ombicademy since its inception in 2115. He'd never been entirely comfortable with the idea of children fighting in a war, but he knew his place and figured that if children were going to be the first line of defense, having them superbly trained would be a good start.

Major Sanders was a tall man who had a face that was often described as "wolfish." His light-blue eyes stayed focused when he spoke, but held the weight of the heavy decisions he had made in his life. He looked like a man who was twenty years older than his forty-eight years, with the deep lines of a stressful life creasing his face and a head of completely gray hair.

He had been sleeping in the privacy of his quarters on the upper levels of the Ombicademy when the transmission came through.

"Three months and they are still restricting him that much?

Have they let up at all?" the dark figure replied in an eerily distorted voice.

Major Sanders had gotten used to this type of communication. The figure on the other end was his contact on Aeris VII, the capitol planet of the *Independents*, the organization of outer colony leaders who wanted to be free from the United Earth Defense Force's oppressive reign.

Sanders had been surprised when the dark figure, which he had taken to calling "The Shadow," had contacted him after the incident of 2115. The Shadow had known details about Sander's life, including his sympathy to the rebellion of the colonies. Of course, the media never mentioned any rebellion, instead focusing on a fictitious war with an alien power. They began working together on a plan that Major Sanders wasn't entirely sure he understood, but it clearly revolved around the prodigy brothers, Connor and Alex Pereira.

"He has been cut off from the training rooms, still performs weekly techno-psychological evaluations, and has even been barred from arena battles until the other students have caught up to his progress with the OMBI. At the rate they're going, it could be another year before Connor sees any progress. To make matters worse, he's still conflicted over his brother's disappearance, and according to the evaluation report, believes Alex was either captured or has turned on the UEDF."

Alex Pereira had been promoted a year prior to graduation of the Ombicademy to lead a special mission to the Eagle Nebula colony, which had sent out a distress signal several months before. It was on that mission that Alex had learned of the *Independents* and of the manipulation of the 4th OMBI inhibitor chip, which caused him to perceive rebel vessels as Gortha ships. He alone turned the tide of the battle of the Eagle Nebula, destroying or capturing the entire convey, including Black Squadron, the UEDF's first OMBI-Enhanced regiment.

"That is unacceptable, Major. Connor needs to be allowed to continue his progress. It is far too important. Besides, we cannot act against the UEDF while they have him," the distorted voice said, with a hint of concern.

"Is one boy so important to the entire fate of the galaxy?" Sanders asked skeptically, not sure what to expect for an answer.

"He is."

"Then I will do what I can. It may take some time for me to convince the Head Commander, but I will get it done."

"Have you received any information on Connor's ship?" The Shadow asked curiously.

No one was sure where he had acquired it, but Connor Pereira had escaped the Ombicademy aboard a Battle Suit Vessel called *Hati* and managed to pilot it all the way to the Eagle Nebula in search of his brother. During his evaluation, Connor had claimed that he found it by going through one of the training rooms into a different part of the academy, where it was waiting for him. No one had believed him.

"The last I heard it was taken to another base for study. Apparently it's remarkably similar to the artifact they had found when they first unlocked the Ombicademy six years ago. I think Harruhama is regretting sending *Skoll* on the Eagle Nebula mission now, since Alex used it to annihilate his top squadron."

"No doubt, Major. *Skoll* is a remarkable feat of engineering, so you understand why the EMC having *Hati* would be of concern. Keep your ears open for further information. If it is anything like *Skoll*, I believe that, by now, only Connor will be able to pilot it."

"I understand. Is there anything else?" Sanders asked, anxiously. Normally his reports were brief and this conversation was the longest he had ever had with The Shadow.

"Yes, one thing." The voice paused a moment for a deep

breath, then continued, "Has Connor learned about the fate of William Mercer?"

William Mercer had been an architect of some repute in Northern California. He had been married to Connor's mother, Captain Marlena Mercer, and had adopted both Connor and Alex soon after the wedding. After her death had been reported in 2115, Alex had joined the Ombicademy and William was left to raise Connor alone. To his credit, the man raised Connor to the best of his ability and helped shape the boy into the prodigy he had become.

William Mercer had been reported deceased three months prior in an explosion at his home during an EMC investigation, which also killed twenty members of a special operations task force.

"Not yet. He's tried to send several messages to him, but he cannot get through. He seems worried, but no one has had the heart to tell him that his stepfather has been killed."

Major Sanders had met William Mercer once and held the man in high regard for his unyielding character and love of his adopted sons. Despite being threatened once by him, he held feelings of regret upon hearing of William's death. The dark figure on the other side of the screen also seemed unsettled each time that Sanders had brought it up.

"I understand," The Shadow replied after an uncharacteristically long pause. "I think he is going to have to find out soon though."

"I know, I will tell him," Sanders replied, not looking forward to the conversation he would have to have with Connor.

"Thank you, Edmond," The Shadow said, using his first name for the first time that Sanders could remember. The transmission ended shortly after, leaving Major Edmond Sanders alone with a sense of anxiety. He had grown to like Connor Pereira, and the idea of delivering heart-breaking news made Sanders feel awful.

He looked at his clock, glowing softly in the darkness; it read 0300. The man returned to his bed, but would not find sleep again that night.

⁓

High in the mountains of Aeris VII, near a communications array built for long-range transmissions, Captain Marlena Mercer was unsuccessfully fighting back her anguish. Tears fell from her almond-colored eyes over her smooth olive skin. Her black hair flowed in the mountain air down the back of her thin, muscular body as she mourned the loss of her husband. She had known that her transmission with Major Sanders would be difficult, as they had been every time since she learned of the death of William Mercer, but she hadn't been prepared for how badly the reminder of him would feel.

William had won her over with a smile eleven years before. His dark-blue eyes always had a way of looking into her as if he were looking at the most majestic sight he had ever seen. When he spoke, he would intelligently articulate concepts she had never thought of before and together they would explore the meaning of existence and the passion of love.

She had been a young mother of two back in those days, and William fit the family equation like he had been born for the job. He loved her boys more than she believed anyone ever could, patiently teaching them about life, self-worth, and the multitude of other subjects he knew. In her mind, she was watching her husband play with her two young sons in the yard, laughing and sharing the enjoyment of their existence. The thought only caused more tears to come. It had been more than six years since she'd seen the man, but she never let go of the love that she had for him.

For more than five years, Marlena had led the

Independents. Having prevented the UEDF attack on the Colonization Freighter Andromeda in the Incident of 2115, the colonists of Aeris VII quickly nominated and elected her as their leader. The attack had been intended to destroy her and the colonists, in order to install the Earth Military Council into a position of galactic power. She had thwarted the attack, killed the men sent to murder her, and had even convinced the UEDF third and fifth fleets to side with her cause.

She had become the EMC martyr, a well-decorated mother of two, the perfect figurehead for the seizure of political power on Earth. Although she had survived the attack, the global media and the EMC reported her death at the hands of the Gortha and, using her popularity as a hero, usurped the civilian government. She had been living in secret ever since, for the safety of her husband and two children back on Earth.

In the early days, she'd tried to get to Earth to reach them but nearly was killed a second time for the effort. She resolved to bide her time, to lay out a plan and eventually get her family to safety. It was she who had Connor drafted to the Ombicademy; with a sympathizer inside she knew her boys would be safe there and eventually she would have the opportunity to reunite with them.

Marlena walked over a grassy hill to where she had landed her ship, the Anubis Class Fighter, *Tizona.* Normally even a pilot of exceptional skill required the help of a navigator and gunner in order to operate an Anubis Fighter; however, Marlena had made many personal modifications to her ship and was renowned for her reputation as both an engineer and the best pilot the UEDF had ever produced. The ship's red alloy frame was a stark contrast to the yellow mountain grasses and the purplish sky beyond.

As she boarded the *Tizona* through the open cargo bay door, Marlena steadied herself by taking several deep breaths.

She knew there would be more tears ahead of her, but for now, she had to focus on events she could control. She closed the cargo bay door with a press of a button on the wall and proceeded up a short flight of stairs through an airlock into the crew quarters. Normally, an Anubis Fighter had a crew of three, with the ability to transport a squad of soldiers in the cargo bay as well, but Marlena, able to fully operate her modified ship, had removed the navigator and gunner quarters, instead making a larger cabin for herself.

The cabin reminded Marlena of being at home. She had covered the cold metal walls with wood planks and added a large bed, which was left unmade while she was awake. The walls were decorated with pictures of her family, all several years old. She even hung curtains over a small porthole, which currently looked out across the heavily treed mountains of the Grimnir Mountain Range on Aeris VII's larger continent.

She spent only a moment in her cabin, looking at a picture of William and Connor sitting on a couch together before continuing through the small kitchen and up to the flight deck, where she powered *Tizona* up for the flight back down to Sapphire City, 30 short minutes away.

As her ship powered up, Marlena opened a secure communication channel and began to broadcast.

"*Tizona* to *Skoll*; *Mephisto*, are you there?" Marlena said in the communicator, with a slight smile on her face at the mere thought of being able to communicate with her eldest son again.

It had been three months since she reunited with her firstborn son, after six years of being apart. Their reunion had been a mix of tears and laughter as they spent day after day reconnecting and sharing their experiences. Marlena had been amazed by how much Alex had grown. When she last saw him, he was a sweet little boy who always had a knack for cooling her off when she got mad. He still had the sweet green eyes and quick smile of the child she remembered, but he'd grown much taller than her and his well-muscled frame gave him a sense of grace and strength.

"Hey, Mom," Alex's voice replied cheerfully over the communicator. "Are you coming back already?"

The reunion had been the happiest event in Marlena's life, in the past six years. It was dimmed quickly when they learned of William's death, and the two had cried together for days. They were also both worried about Connor and, together, worked tirelessly to modify plans on how to pull him out of the Ombicademy, so that they could reunite the family once and for all.

"Affirmative, returning to Sapphire just as soon as these engines warm up; ETA thirty minutes," Marlena replied, matching Alex's cheerful tone as best she could.

"Is everything okay?" Alex asked, sounding sincerely concerned.

Apparently, she hadn't done as good a job matching his cheer as she had hoped, or Alex was as perceptive to her mood as he had been when he was younger. She was grateful to have her son back in her life. It gave her pleasure beyond words to know he was waiting for her in their house in Sapphire City, the capital of Aeris VII. But she knew she was going to have to share Sanders' report and hated the idea of Alex crying even one more tear.

"We'll talk when I get back. I'll give you the full report then," she said absently, trying to avoid saying more than she had to over the communicator.

"Affirmative, see you in thirty minutes, Mom."

Tizona lifted easily off the grassy plateau and up into the light-purple sky of Aeris VII. It was the planet that was meant to be the epicenter of UEDF activity in the Hourglass Nebula and a hub for trade between the colonies. After the incident of 2115, Marlena arrested the EMC leaders assigned to the colony and declared independence from Earth. As she flew over the long valleys and wide rivers, Marlena marveled, as she always had, at what a paradise Aeris VII was, especially compared to some of the other colonies.

The planet was about half of the size of Earth with water covering most of the surface. Two continents sat on opposite sides of the planet, both blessed with fertile land, temperate climates and an abundance of fresh water. The hugh of the sky was the result of a slightly denser upper atmosphere which also caused Aeris' two moons to appear violet and crimson in the sky.

The entire population of the planet was only about twenty thousand people, which represented the original colonists and crew of the Andromeda, the crew and families of the 3rd and 5th fleets as well as various other colonists from other systems who had wanted to relocate. Most of those people lived in the city, although many had chosen to build homes and smaller settlements within short flying distance of the capital.

The flight from the communications array to Sapphire City went by in a dreamy haze, Marlena thinking a lot about her family, trying to come up with a good plan to reconnect with her youngest son.

As she came out of the Grimnir Mountains, she spotted the city beyond. Sapphire was a beautiful place, having been built strictly using the commanding architectural concepts pioneered by William Mercer. The buildings and homes were all structurally designed as tributes to the materials they were built with, every square foot of ground well-planned and carefully designed for the optimum balance of function and flow. Everything about Sapphire was majestic. The city only housed about twelve thousand people, most living near the edge of a great lake they called Amsvartnir. The city only had eight tall buildings, which were used mostly for commerce at street level and apartments above. On the far end of the city, opposite the lake, sat the planet's only military controlled airfield, where several frigates were undergoing maintenance for their turn in the rotation of orbital defense patrols.

Marlena aimed *Tizona* at a small island that was a little over two miles off the coast of the city and set her down on a landing pad behind a large house that stood as the island's only structure.

She had built the house there with the help of the Aeris colonists, which they described as a "temple to the woman's fiery spirit." It was as large as the home she had back in Healdsburg, California, and built with a similar style in mind. Naturally Marlena had given it a more fiery touch, emphasizing the raw energy of nature in its concept, unlike the home that William had designed back on Earth. His design flowed with the landscape in the valley, where it had stood, using the curvature of the land to emphasize his design. By contrast, Marlena's design dominated the island and the lake around it. Using strong lightweight metals and force field generators as design materials, the house stood in defiance of nature as if challenging the heavens themselves to try to remove it from the island.

The fortifications had a practical purpose more than an aesthetic one, even though Aeris VII rarely produced a storm that would threaten even the weakest structure. The house was built to withstand an orbital attack for a short time as well as any atmospheric bombardment; as the leader of the *Independents*, Marlena knew that she had to take extra precautions from assassination attempts.

Tizona settled onto the platform at the rear of the house, next to where *Skoll* knelt like a dragon-faced samurai in black armor, bowing before his lord. Marlena was surprised to see Alex outside washing his Battle Armor Vessel with a rag and bucket. She smiled at the apparent care he was taking in making sure that his ship looked immaculate.

Although, more than twenty feet tall while standing, kneeling *Skoll* was much smaller than *Tizona* and, as they discovered after the Battle of the Eagle Nebula, could actually fit into *Tizona's* cargo hold. After powering her ship down, Marlena disembarked through the cargo hold doors and met her son on the landing pad.

Alex was only sixteen, but he had grown into a man with the body of an athlete. Standing over six feet tall, his strong arms and legs gave him the appearance of an adult rather than a teenage boy. He kept his hair short, which emphasized his striking green eyes and the fluid handsomeness of his face. He wore a tank top that morning, showing off his muscular arms and the glowing black bracer that he always wore on his right wrist.

Looking at Alex, Marlena was glad that she kept her home on an island, if only so that the teenage girls in Sapphire City wouldn't beat down her door to get her son. He had already earned a reputation for his heroics in the Battle of the Eagle Nebula and, in town, Alex was something of a minor celebrity.

"How did it go, Mom?" Alex asked, cutting right to the point.

"Not bad. Major Sanders is working on the plan, but it's going to take some time."

"What's the problem then? Is Tons okay?"

"He is. They're giving him a hard time and I don't know how he's going to react when he hears the news about William."

"Yeah, they were really close. I don't know if he will ever get over it," Alex said insightfully, deep concern evident in his voice.

"I know. I'm worried about it too, but if either one of us tries to get anywhere close to Earth now, we're going to be attacked by the full force of the UEDF."

Alex unconsciously looked over at *Skoll*. With the help of his mom, he had defeated two UEDF Battle Frigates and the entirety of Black Squadron, capturing most of the pilots. Even so, he knew he would be overwhelmed near Earth, even with the help of the powerful Battle Suit Vessel.

"Don't even think about it, Alex! You would get close, I have no doubt. But the orbital defenses around Earth are way too strong. Even if we went in with everything we had, none of us would make it home."

"I know!" Alex snapped, anger burning in his eyes.

Marlena was shocked to see her son so upset. Normally Alex had a cool head, choosing to remain calm and focused rather than displaying fierce anger. Connor burned hot, Marlena was like a wildfire, but Alex was like a cool lake with a calm surface.

"I can see you're upset," Marlena began, not used to seeing her son at all reactive, "but we need to bide our time. I have been getting reports that Harruhama has begun imprisoning influential UEDF dissenters, from bloggers to public figures. Gas prices are rising and even people who have been found stockpiling weapons and food have been under investigation. The situation on Earth is bad, and the EMC may soon lose control."

"I know. I just can't stand waiting while Connor is still out there. I'm worried that Harruhama won't give up on coming after the colonies too. With Earth's resources so depleted, I don't think we can expect peaceful negotiation anytime soon," Alex said, calming down.

Marlena was amazed at how well-informed Alex was. He had been paying attention during the strategy sessions he'd attended, sharing information with the best minds in the 3rd and 5th fleets. His eye for political influence and military tactics was incredible.

"Well, there isn't anything more we can do about it for today. We have to trust our men on the inside and focus on the problems we can solve. If things get bad enough on Earth, we will make a move. Until then, we wait."

"I know. I just worry about Connor. We have to bring him back here, Mom," Alex said, sounding sincerely worried.

Marlena was touched by her son's concern and shared much of what he felt. She had felt impatient every day for the past six years, wanting to get a chance at recovering her children. When she received word from Adam Malavich, of Atmos XI, that Connor had come looking for his brother just after they'd left, she cursed and threw things for the better part of the day until Alex calmed her down.

Now looking at her oldest son, she calmed down again. She knew that if they worked together, they could find a way to get to Connor. With that thought in mind, she took her son inside to make him dinner.

CHAPTER 2

Will to Power

CONNOR WOKE UP THE MORNING OF THE BATTLE ON his bunk in the Green Army barracks feeling depressed. He hated the idea of sitting on the sidelines while the other kids were gaining skills and points to unlock valuable weapons and abilities on their OMBIs. He had even been banned from using the practice rooms, which had all been welded shut before he was even allowed back into the Ombicademy. To make matters worse, he hadn't been able to send or receive mail from William or Alex in months, leaving him feeling entirely alone. He still went to the gym every day, hoping to catch a glimpse of one of his friends from Blue Army; however, no matter what time he went, the gym was nearly empty when he arrived.

He was frustrated watching his new army go out to a battle, knowing they would probably lose without him, while he had to remain in the barracks. He had been waiting like this for months, hoping he would get a chance to get back into the arena or training rooms soon. Connor Pereira did not like stagnating.

When his OMBI vibrated with new mail, Connor got extremely excited for a moment, hoping that it was from his family. His excitement was crushed a moment later when he read the message:

Message 1: Report to Observation Lounge "Conscript Pereira is ordered to report to the observation lounge immediately." delivered 0800 2121-07-03 From: Major Sanders

Connor dressed in his green uniform frowning the entire time. He had been the commander of Blue Army when he first arrived at the battle school five months prior. His record was still undefeated; however, the new Head Commander had removed the scoreboard and transferred him to Green Army as just a soldier, a soldier who was not allowed to fight. Connor hated his green uniform; it always reminded him that he wasn't a part of the army that he'd started out on, never mind his OMBI was still blue when he used it.

He walked slowly through the cold metal halls of the Ombicademy, taking the longest way possible to get where he was going. He walked by the Blue Army barracks, hoping to run into one of his friends, but was disappointed to find out they had gone to the commissary. He passed by the now-sealed training rooms where he had met Omega, the training hologram that taught him how to fight and eventually led him to *Hati*, the Battle Suit Vessel that took him to the Eagle Nebula. Connor grimaced at the memory; he never thought he would miss hanging out with a simulated person.

Leaving his old barracks and training rooms behind, he walked until he arrived at the lift to the observation deck, thinking about what Major Sanders could possibly want with him. When the airman at the lift asked him why he was there, Connor went into a tirade.

"I was summoned, obviously. How efficient is it that every time there's an order issued, the peons don't hear about it and have to ask everyone who walks by what they are doing? Never mind, you won't know, since you obviously don't know anything!"

The airman was stunned by the child's outburst, and without another word stepped aside to allow Connor access to the lift. Getting aboard and pushing the button for the observation lounge, Connor glared at the airman until the doors had sealed shut. Riding up the lift, Connor could see his reflection in the metal doors and was surprised at how different he looked compared to when he had first been drafted.

His once-foppish hair had been cut short, more befitting a soldier. He had grown a little bit over the last five months too, he could tell because the uniform he wore felt tight and looked a little too small. The bracer attached to his arm didn't hurt anymore at least, just felt like a part of his arm now. But it was his eyes that had changed most; not being allowed to participate in battle or train, Connor's eyes had lost their spark. He looked away from the reflection and grumbled about how lift technology should be improved to go a little faster.

When he got to the top, the doors opened slowly, revealing the anteroom of the observation lounge. The administrator stood behind a metal desk, starring down at Connor as if she were about to tell him to go back downstairs. Before she could speak, Connor saved her the trouble.

"Connor Pereira here to see Major Sanders," he said quickly.

"Have a seat," the administrator said, pointing to some chairs on the far side of the room.

"No." Connor walked past her through the doors to the observation room.

He hadn't felt like taking a suggestion just then from some administrator. He figured that adults always thought they could tell kids what to do, just because they were bigger. But ever since he had mastered martial arts in the training room and had piloted a Battle Armor Vessel across the galaxy, Connor didn't feel like he was smaller than anybody.

The administrator objected, but lost the argument when

Connor shut the doors behind him, locking them with a deft turn of his left hand. With a mischievous grin on his face, Connor turned to find Major Sanders waiting for him.

"You really are a funny kid," the major began, putting Connor off his guard. He hadn't seen the man since he had been recruited more than five months before, but he remembered that Sanders hadn't treated him very well.

"Well, if it isn't the big man who drugs small children in the privacy of his own little airplane," Connor began smugly. "I won't even ask what you did to me while I was asleep."

The smile the major had been wearing was gone. He scowled at Connor as he had done all those months before.

"Now that's the Major Sanders I remember," Connor said with a grin.

"Look down there," Sanders ordered, changing the subject.

He pointed out one of the arenas, where Black Army was making short work of Green Army class 2126.

"Green Army is a bunch of babies. They can't beat Black Army," Connor said after looking down at the battle raging below.

"No one else can either."

"I can! It was easy too. Blue Army completely shut them out," Connor replied, remembering his first battle with the supposedly unbeatable Black Army.

"Since your last victory, no one has been able to challenge Black Army in the arena," Sanders informed Connor. It wasn't really news to the boy; he had suspected that Blue Army would not do as well without him leading.

"Then maybe you should get all the other armies to team up against them, or was that just for me?"

"That was not my call, but yes, that was the only time in Ombicademy history that more than two armies fought in the arena."

"And because no one could beat me, I am not allowed to fight or train?" Connor asked, venom oozing from his voice.

"Also, not my call, kid, the new Head Commander believes that all soldiers should have an equal chance to grow."

"Except me," Connor corrected.

Major Sanders just shrugged. He agreed with everything Connor said, but didn't have a solution to offer.

"Listen, kid, I didn't invite you up here to listen to you complain about how unfair your life is. I brought you up here because I had something important to tell you," Sanders said, taking control of the conversation.

"Well, what is it?" Connor asked impatiently.

"It's about your stepfather. Three months ago, during a routine investigation, William Mercer, along with twenty members of a special operations team, died in an explosion at your home in Healdsburg."

Silence hung in the air as Connor digested the news. Sanders could see tears beginning to well up at the corners of the kid's eyes as if he were trying to fight back waves of despair. Major Sanders knew how close this boy was to his stepfather, and the idea that he had just delivered news of the third parent that he lost in his short life, left Sanders feeling sick.

Connor burst into tears.

"An explosion that killed twenty-one people during a routine investigation?!" Connor screamed angrily, tears pouring down his cheeks.

"Yeah, kid, that's what the report said," Sanders offered quietly.

"That is a load of crap! What kind of investigation involves twenty spec-ops soldiers?!"

Sanders didn't know what to say. He'd heard the report, but he knew better than to ask too many questions.

"They went there to kill him because he hated the EMC!

Only he must have killed them too! You bastards took my mom, my brother, and now William!" Connor was screaming in hysterics.

"I have nobody!" Connor fell to his knees, sobbing heavily.

"Untrue," a voice said in a whisper.

"What do you mean?" Connor demanded.

Sanders stood staring at him.

"I didn't say anything," he said quietly.

Connor looked around the room, but didn't see anybody else. He cried on the floor for several minutes while Major Sanders watched. The man seemed sympathetic, but at that point nothing was going to make Connor forgive him for bringing him this news.

Gathering himself to his feet, Connor glared at Major Sanders before marching to the door. Throwing the door wide open, he stomped up to the administrator's desk, trying to wipe the tears off his cheeks.

"I would like to make an appointment to see the Head Commander," Connor demanded, tears still falling from his chocolate-colored eyes.

"The Head Commander doesn't take appointments from conscripts," the Administrator informed him with her nose up in the air.

"Well then, when is he in, so I can come by unannounced?" Connor rebutted, finding an immediate hole in the rule.

The Administrator was quiet, staring down at him like he was just any little kid.

"Never mind, you're probably just too stupid to take an appointment," he finished as he walked back to the lift.

Not one to let a thing like rules stop him from his goal, Connor pushed the button on the lift for the Ombicademy Faculty Quarters. He tapped his foot impatiently as the lift descended down one floor and slowed to a stop. The doors opened to reveal a long hallway with several labeled doorways.

The names of the faculty members who lived at the Ombicademy were prominently displayed on each of the doors, making it easy for Connor to find the living quarters of Head Commander, Colonel Franklin Setzer. The door was large and made of dark blue metal; he found it at the very end of a long hallway. He didn't bother knocking.

Colonel Setzer was powerful man, short and muscular. He kept his head shaved completely bald and wore a thick mustache. He had been reading a book when Connor entered his room and didn't bother setting it down as the boy stormed up to his desk.

"It's true what they say; you can open all the doors," Colonel Setzer said smugly, not looking up from his book.

"Head Commander, I am here to demand that you allow me access to train again or at least to battle. I also want to be transferred back to Blue Army."

"Is that so?" Setzer said with a condescending chuckle, still reading from behind his thin glasses.

Connor slapped the man's book out of his hands and onto the floor.

"Yes, that is so!" Connor snapped.

Setzer didn't move to retrieve his book, only stared back at Connor, the smug expression gone from his face.

"I could have you arrested for that." The threat was clear in his tone.

"Just try it and see if you even make it out of the room," the boy replied, making it clear what would happen if the man moved.

Tension filled the room at Connor's words, despite the smile slowly spreading across the Colonel's face. Franklin Setzer was strong and well-trained, even so, he wondered if Connor, even with the limited power of an inhibited OMBI would have much trouble taking him down. Regardless, he had to admire the 10-year-old kid who wasn't backing down in the face of authority, age, and power.

It was with that admiration that had Setzer eventually replying, "I will allow supervised training and a transfer to Blue Army. But I will continue to pick the commanders of the armies."

Connor hesitated only a moment before he backed down.

"Don't keep selling after the sale has been made," William had always told him.

That advice echoing in his head, Connor turned and walked out of the Head Commander's quarters without another word, believing the man would honor his promise.

The Head Commander watched Connor leave. He'd intended to leave Connor with the threat, "If I ever see you in the officers' quarters again, I'll have you shot," but he didn't think the kid would actually care.

For a long while after the exchange, Head Commander Setzer sat thinking about the boy who had stood up to him, and all the ways that he would get back at him.

CHAPTER 3

Beyond Good and Evil

FROM THE PENTHOUSE SUITE OF THE PARK BUILDING IN Chicago, Councilman Kaufmann of the EMC stared out the window at the evening skyline of the windy city with a glass of wine in his hand. He'd been reading reports of the *Independents'* progress in the outer colonies with a frown on his face.

Kaufmann, a blond-haired, German-born politician in his mid-fifties, had spent the last seven years of his reign watching the slow erosion of EMC political power, despite the efforts of media propaganda and the eminent "Gortha" threat. The people had been dissatisfied with the council for a long time, but had never organized or rioted as long as they had the promise of food or reduction of gas prices.

In Germany, the devaluation of global currency, combined with shortages of food and fuel, had caused massive inflation over the last two years, and the recent riots in Berlin had forced Kaufmann to seek the refuge of his second home in Illinois. He had appealed to the council, who agreed to send military aid to Berlin; however, no aid had come. In his haste to escape the country, the councilman had left his wife and daughter behind.

When he'd sent a formal request to General Harruhama for military aid, the man had told him, HIM, that there were no troops to spare with the outer colonies withholding resources. Kaufmann had demanded reports and received them on his datapad an hour later. The "*Independents*" did not seem overly aggressive to Kaufmann, but they had been denying Earth their resources for more than five years, causing shortages in food and energy.

Kaufmann had been writing an angry reply to Harruhama demanding a vote for full-scale military action against the people of Germany when he heard a knock at his door. The sound distracted him slightly, but he went back to his message, hearing one of his bodyguards moving to answer it.

"*General, the situation in Germany is getting worse. Without the full aid of the UEDF International Guard, we will lose the entire country in a matter of weeks. Rioters have seized all government buildings in Berlin and have been pushing back the local forces out of the city. I fear it may be too late—Kaufmann*"

"Who is there?" the bodyguard asked with a thick German accent.

Kaufmann thought he heard someone speaking from the other side of the door, but the sound was muffled. He began to re-read his message, checking to make sure it conveyed the proper sense of urgency.

"Please say again, I cannot hear you," the bodyguard said loudly at the door.

The sound of a large explosion startled the councilman, causing him to drop his datapad. One of his bodyguards flew backwards into the office where Kaufmann was standing, crumpling against the side of a couch in a smoldering heap. The other six bodyguards ran into the room, yelling to each other to take up defensive positions.

Kaufmann's ears rang from the rattle of gunfire; loud, piercing blasts overwhelmed the sound of his bodyguards' handguns. Panicking, Kaufmann ran into his bedroom and pulled a small revolver out of the nightstand before hiding in his closet. The sounds of battle raged on in the entry way of the penthouse for nearly a minute, loud blasts followed by the pops of smaller guns, shaking the walls of the closet. Kaufmann imagined twenty armed men storming his apartment by the sound of the battle.

Finally, the gunfire stopped, the eerie quiet punctuated by the thud of a body falling to the ground. Kaufmann could hear heavy boots stomping through his penthouse as they made their way toward his bedroom. The man let out a soft cry, which brought the boots marching up to where he was hiding.

The doors of the closet swung open and, before Kaufmann could take a shot, a gloved hand grabbed his arm and pulled him hard onto the floor. Kaufmann turned in terror and was shocked to see that only one man had entered his room, one terrifying man.

He stood nearly six feet tall, wearing heavy black boots and thick blue jeans. The jeans were torn slightly from bullet holes, revealing the mechanized battle armor underneath; armor normally only worn by EMC Operatives. The man's leather duster flowed out behind him as he leveled Kaufmann with a fist to the face. Kaufmann rolled back toward the window of his bedroom, looking down on the city below. The man came on, grabbing the councilman by his neck and lifting him up against the window so they were face to face.

The man's nose and mouth were covered by a red bandana, and a black cowboy hat gave him the look of a western outlaw. As imposing as his outfit was, what terrified Kaufmann the most was the man's steel-blue eyes, cold and merciless, the eyes of death himself.

"Wha … what do you want?" Kaufmann managed to sputter.

"I want the truth." The man's voice was ice. It caused Kaufmann's spine to shiver.

"The truth about what?"

"The incident of 2115. Speak quick."

"My datapad has everything you need. Please don't kill me."

"Your datapad will be traced and you know it. You really are a clever little weasel, aren't you? Besides, I didn't follow you all the way from Berlin to read a datapad. Tell me the truth!" The man glared straight into Kaufmann's eyes like he was looking for him to speak a lie.

"You were in Berlin?" Kaufmann asked, realizing the gravity of the situation. "You had something to do with the riots?"

"Send the dogs in and the birds will fly. Now tell me what I want to know!" the man demanded, his eyes flashing.

"Okay, I will tell you everything! We were losing control of the people; we were out of resources! We had to protect ourselves, don't you understand? It was for the greater good!"

"Then it's true. The entire thing was a lie in order to seize power. The Gortha aren't real."

"It was Harruhama's idea! We had to…"

Kaufmann felt the man's fingers begin to tighten around his throat. Gasping for breath, he tried to fight back, but wasn't strong enough. Before his vision went totally black, he felt the window crack behind him mere moments before he was greeted with the terrifying sense of falling.

—

The holotube news would call it an "act of terrorism by Gortha sympathizers," in order to convince the people around the world to rally around their leaders. The man that they would label "The Dragoon" was pictured as a crazed cowboy with wild hair and consumed by bloodlust. Images were released from a lobby camera of the man carrying a strange-looking three-barreled shotgun, and the report included statistics on the dozens of innocent people who were murdered in the gun fight.

In his office, General Harruhama wondered what information the councilman might have given up before he met his end at the hands of the psychopathic vigilante. The general had his men check the datapad, but they found no trace of any information reviewed or any DNA samples to draw from.

Trying to track a man using low-tech gear, with no traceable implants and no communication devices, would be difficult. Harruhama was not naïve enough to believe that he had heard the last of the name *Dragoon*. That disturbing thought in his head, he tapped his communicator.

"Yes, sir?" the administrator said on the other end of the line.

"Get me the council on video immediately."

"Yes, sir."

Four minutes later, Harruhama was in a conference with the other seven surviving members of the Earth Military Council.

"Fellow councilmen and women," Harruhama began formally, "today a great travesty has occurred. We have lost our dear brother, Councilman Kaufmann, in an attack against the EMC itself!"

"Do we know who is really responsible for the attack?" Councilwoman Singh of India began. "The media report spoke of a crazed western-folk villain."

"The media has reported it as we know it, Councilwoman Singh. Our details on the motivation behind the attack and the faction responsible are limited. No documents or information were stolen and no politically motivated message was left at the scene."

"Is the rest of the council in any danger?" Councilman Namgung of Korea asked, his forehead beading with sweat.

"We have no reason to suspect that any of us are in danger.

It may have been a personal vendetta against Kaufmann; the riots in Germany did cause the man to flee, leaving his family behind."

"Just in case, I think we should all increase our personal security," Councilwoman Morgan of the United Kingdom said quietly.

"Agreed," the rest replied in unison.

"What is the plan on dealing with the assassin then, General?" Councilwoman Singh asked quietly.

"I have my top staff working on a way to get the true identity of this 'Dragoon.' Once we have it, we can establish his patterns and prevent any further activity."

"Have any of our surveillance systems picked up his movements around Chicago?" Singh continued.

"No, we only have him going in and out of the Park Building, nothing after," Harruhama replied.

"What about before?" Singh asked, inquisitively.

"We have some footage of the man in Berlin outside of Kaufmann's residence and some of the government buildings as far back as three weeks ago. It would appear that the Dragoon had something to do with the riots and probably chose Kaufmann because of his weak grip on the people of his region."

"I understand; thank you, General," Councilwoman Singh finished.

"Any further business?" Harruhama asked to the assembled EMC.

"We have received your report regarding the rebel fleet movements around the Aeris Colony, General. Is it your contention that in six days they will be vulnerable?" Councilman Stahl of the United States asked politely.

"It is, Councilman Stahl. Our reports come from an agent in place at the colony, an operative who has been assigned to identify and eliminate rebel leaders."

"Unfortunately, it will take months for a battle group to get out that far, otherwise we could end this rebellion quickly," Stahl stated.

"I ordered the battle group out two months ago when I first received this information."

"Without council approval, General?" Stahl asked, the accusation clear in his words.

"Indeed. I had to act and could not wait for the declaration by the council. I trust that no one objects?"

The council was silent, no one daring to cross Harruhama publicly. None of them were certain that it wasn't one of Harruhama's own operatives that killed Kaufmann, instead of this masked vigilante they had been led to believe.

"What is the status of the military support for the Germany riots?" Councilman Moreau of France asked. "They are nearing the border of my region."

"At this time, Councilman, the EMC is unable to divert military support to a regional problem. Local troops will have to suffice. The lack of resources coming in from the outer colonies takes precedence."

"Then what of Germany?" Moreau asked quietly.

"We leave it to its own destruction," Harruhama said, his expression blank, impassive.

When the conference ended, General Harruhama quietly pondered his decisions. He didn't like the idea of giving up on Germany; however, one hundred and twenty-five million fewer mouths to feed would definitely take some of the pressure off of the food reserves. The best scientists and soldiers from that region were already drafted into military service, so if the people of Germany wanted to kill themselves, Harruhama would not stop them.

In the end, it was an easy decision for General Harruhama to make.

⌒

Deep in space, the seven Battle Frigates of the 2nd Fleet were emerging from their slipstream fold into the Hourglass Nebula. Standard slipstream jumps were never as accurate as Commander Balvoon of the UEDF Frigate Cortez had liked, but this particular jump had landed him and his battle group within a week of their target.

Commander Balvoon had been chosen to lead this strike against the diminished forces of Aeris VII who had been rallying the other colonies behind the banner of the *Independents*. His service record and unquestioning loyalty to the UEDF made Balvoon the perfect man to handle the rebel leaders he was to identify and execute if possible.

They had received a report two months prior that the enemy fleet movements had left them spread thin around the Colonies' capital world, and General Harruhama, who had issued the order himself, believed that the seven Battle Frigates would be enough to wipe out every last colonist, if necessary.

The battle group formed up around the UEDF Cortez and proceeded toward Aeris VII with all possible speed.

CHAPTER 4

Cerulean Skies

O<small>N A COOL CLOUDY MORNING,</small> C<small>APTAIN</small>
Alexzander Pereira looked out over the choppy
waters of Lake Amsvartnir toward the city beyond.
He leaned casually against a column, letting his hands absorb
the warmth of the cup of coffee he held reverently. He'd never
been much of a coffee drinker on Earth, but the coffee that
grew in the hills nearby, like all the food on Aeris VII, was
incredible.

A cool breeze blew off the lake, and as he felt it caress
his skin he closed his eyes and let his mind roll back over the
months and years to a time when he stood on another porch,
similar to the one he stood on now, staring at his brother and
stepfather chasing each other around in the yard.

In his mind, Alex watched William, who was pretending
to be a zombie, chase Connor around in the grass while dragging one leg and groaning. It was a fun memory in Alex's life,
watching his brother laughing and playing. He had been a little
old for it then, but always kind of wished in his heart that he
could be chased around too.

As William closed the distance, Connor emulated pulling
a pin out of a grenade and threw at him. William went down

with his best version of a zombie scream and continued to crawl after Connor as if he had no legs.

The "crawler," as Connor called it, was the most terrifying version of the zombie chase for him. Alex never knew why; he could casually walk away from the biting mouth and grasping claws, but for some reason, Connor was even more afraid of it. Later, when Alex asked William why it was so scary for Connor, William had said, "Because that's the point in the chase when he finds out that the monster will never stop coming."

Alex smiled at the thought from all those years ago and found himself wearing a similar smile now, while staring out over the lake. Tears rimmed the boy's eyes as the feeling washed over him that he would never be able to share those games with the man again and that his brother was still out there in the galaxy, alone and struggling, while Alex was safe with their mom.

Marlena came out of the house then wearing a thick wool robe and carrying a steaming cup of coffee, joining her son on the porch.

"Good morning," she said, her soft voice betraying a hint of concern for him.

"Good morning, Mom."

"What's the matter?" She read his emotions like she was reading a book.

"I miss him," Alex said, choosing to not elaborate on who he meant, not wanting to see his mother cry again.

"Me too," she replied, her voice barely a whisper.

The boy and his mother stood leaning against each other, sharing a moment of silence for the one they had lost. The small waves lapped against the shore of the island below the deck, and as they listened to the rhythmic song, they both lost themselves in memories.

After a minute, Marlena broke the reverie by clearing her throat.

"You've been cooped up in this house for days, why don't you go into the city? You can take the boat and walk around."

"I guess so." Alex shrugged.

"Don't give me any of that. Just go and try to enjoy yourself. You know, the people here know who you are and what you did in the Eagle Nebula. They all think of you as a hero."

"Really?" Alex asked, feigning surprise as he tried to hide a grin.

"Yes really. All the schools are out this time of year; why don't you go see if you can make some friends?"

"Okay, do you want to come with me?"

"I can't, I have a conference with the 3rd and 5th fleet commanders later regarding where to deploy ships to help the more distressed colonies."

"That sounds awesome. Have fun!" Alex quipped with a smile.

Marlena shrugged. She knew there was a lot of work in leading the *Independents* and accepted the role gracefully. Deep in her heart she understood that she was the most qualified person to lead and she accepted the role, knowing that if she wanted her children to know real freedom in their lifetime, she would have to continue to fight.

Alex spent the better part of an hour showering and getting dressed for town. It had been a long time since he'd worn anything but a single-piece uniform and was glad that his mom had picked him up some civilian clothes.

His room in this house was not entirely unlike his room back in Healdsburg, before it exploded. He had two captain's beds and a desk between them. The room even had children's toys put away on a shelf, which made Alex miss his brother. His mom had obviously designed it to feel like home, and had clearly been waiting for a long time to be able to bring her sons there.

He picked out a pair of white plaid shorts, white tennis shoes, and a T-shirt, which had a snug fit. It was a little cold out on the water so he also elected to grab a gray hooded sweatshirt before walking downstairs and out the back door.

The dock was a short walk from the deck down a flight of wooden stairs. Moored there was a large black and red speed-boat, which he grinned at as he went about untying the ropes before climbing aboard. Alex had never driven a boat in his life, but found an option for general watercraft on his OMBI that he unlocked.

It still surprised Alex that the OMBI no longer required him to use points to purchase any upgrades; instead, it had a long green bar across the top of the display. The bar diminished slightly when he unlocked the boat and then slowly began to expand back out to the edges of the virtual display. The change came after Alex removed the fourth inhibitor chip during the battle of the Eagle Nebula.

The point system and battle statistics had been a function of that chip, along with the ability for the UEDF to alter the wearer's perception. In that battle, Alex had been unable to see the rebel ships as anything but Gortha fighters. He could sense the alterations in his own mind, which prompted him to have the inhibitor removed. It had all been a revelation to Alex about the lengths the UEDF would go to manipulate its soldiers, and the civilian population for that matter. William had always told him that the media was a propaganda machine, but until recently Alex never took any of it very seriously.

Piloting the speedboat as if he had been raised living near the water, Alex set a course for the harbor on the far side of the lake and sped along, enjoying the feeling of mist and wind in his face.

⌒

Marlena watched the low clouds engulf the mountains around Lake Amsvartnir as she listened to the boat pull away from the dock. She had been enjoying her son's company every day, but was glad to see him off exploring, hoping that he would get some enjoyment out of socializing in town.

It had been more than six weeks since they came out of their slipstream jump to Aeris VII. After the fact, Alex told her that *Skoll*'s slipstream lost a lot less time in between jumps than *Tizona*'s; they resolved to use his drive when traveling together in the future. The more time that passed between jumps, the more time they would miss in between. Marlena had been jumping through slipstreams so much in her role as leader of the rebellion that she had only actually aged about three years of the last six that had occurred.

She understood the effects of folding time and space well, having studied it at length during her days as a military pilot. No matter how much understanding she had or preparation she made, she never felt comfortable with the perception that the people around her were aging almost twice as fast as she was. When she first saw Alex again, it had felt like the ten-year-old boy he was should have aged about three years, which she had been ready for; the sixteen-year-old boy who greeted her came as a shock. Her kids grew up too fast under normal circumstances and she was not happy about the idea of them growing up any faster than that.

Marlena walked through the quiet halls of her home from the kitchen, where she had started a fresh pot of coffee, to the study where she had many documents and monitors displaying a variety of statistics. From ship repair progress to patrol schedules, the information scrolled across the screen, giving her, the leader of the *Independents,* as much information as possible to make informed decisions.

She spent a lot of time in her study when she was on the planet, giving most of her attention to the details of the war, often thinking about the man who sat in a similar study, more than eight thousand light years away. She put the thought out of her mind before it could consume her. She knew that the house she imagined was gone, and so was the man.

Turning her focus to war assets, she began reading the updated numbers:

UEDF Assets:
Fleet 1 (28 active Battle Frigates, 6 Anubis Squadrons)
Fleet 2 (25 active Battle Frigates, 5 Anubis Squadrons)
Fleet 6 (20 active Battle Frigates, 4 Anubis Squadrons)
Fleet 7 (20 active Battle Frigates, 4 Anubis Squadrons)
Fleet 8 (25 active Battle Frigates, 5 Anubis Squadrons)

Independent Assets:
Fleet 3 (18 active Battle Frigates, 2 Anubis Squadrons)
Fleet 5 (24 active Battle Frigates, 4 Anubis Squadrons)

The balance of power didn't inspire confidence in Marlena. She knew the UEDF had other assets as well, including more than one hundred and sixty OMBI-enhanced soldiers from the Ombicademy who were about to graduate. Her data didn't show minor vessels, like RA Fighters, or orbital defensive structures. But she knew those figures read like the fleet numbers.

In a head-to-head military engagement, her fleets were severely outgunned. However, she knew that the EMC would not risk that kind of an engagement yet. When fleet 3 had defected with her after the 2115 incident, Harruhama sent fleets 4 and 5 to destroy them. The battle group commander of the 5th fleet had known Marlena as an honorable soldier and a friend, so when it came time to attack, the 5th fleet defected as well. The battle turned quickly and regrettably; the entirety of the 4th fleet was destroyed in the process.

Before her meeting with her commanders, she updated the list of assets to include the *Tizona* and *Skoll*. The former was possibly stronger than any two squads of Anubis fighters combined, especially with Marlena piloting the modified ship. The latter was possibly stronger than any ten Battle Frigates, the way it moved fluidly throughout the battlefield. Alex was an amazing pilot, and the battle of the Eagle Nebula had turned very quickly when he joined in; Black Squadron, the preeminent battle group of the UEDF, went down in under two minutes.

Noticing the time, Marlena activated her communication console and saw that the Independent Council of Colonies (ICC) had already convened. They had been waiting patiently for her; she never missed a session when she was on the planet to participate.

"Greetings, Captain Mercer, are you ready to begin?" asked the friendly voice of Nathaniel Watson, Commander of the 3rd fleet.

The Independent Council of Colonies was the military body of alliance between the outer colonies. It was led by Marlena and four other members including the two fleet commanders of the 3rd and 5th fleets, an elected civilian representative of Aeris VII and the former Captain of the Colonization Freighter Andromeda, Armando Velez.

"I apologize if I was late, Commander Watson. Let us begin."

"No apology necessary, Captain. How are things with your son?"

Marlena smiled as she replied, "Nice of you to ask, Commander. Our reunion has been wonderful."

"Glad to hear it. Now that we're all here we have two major

items and two minor items that need to be resolved. Commander Clarke, go ahead." Commander Watson said taking the lead.

The commander of the 5th fleet began, "Thank you, Commander; also, I have to say, it's nice to see you back planet side, Captain Mercer. We are spread thin defending seventeen colonies with only forty-two frigates total, between the 3rd and 5th fleets. With the addition of Atmos XI, we are unable to heavily fortify the Capital with more than five frigates and two Anubis Squads."

"That is not a problem with *Skoll* and *Tizona* both on Aeris VII. But if we go off world, we will be vulnerable here," Marlena chimed in firmly.

"We're trying to develop an early warning system for vessels entering the system using your communication array, but it's slow going. We have also begun to develop orbital defense systems like the ones they have around Earth to discourage any direct assaults," Commander Clarke said, reading from his notes.

"Well, keep at it. Send me the engineering documents for both systems and I will see what I can do to help," Marlena offered.

"Thank you, Captain," Commander Watson said before changing the subject. "The second subject is the status of your other son."

"Connor is being monitored by my agent in the Ombicademy; we are biding our time to wait for the opportunity to retrieve him," Marlena explained.

"I've been reading a report about the *Skoll*'s ability to slip-stream quickly and accurately. Is it possible, in your opinion, to use it to retrieve Connor?" Commander Watson asked, genuinely concerned.

Marlena was shaking her head before Watson finished his question. "I don't believe so. The orbital defenses around Earth make that kind of a mission incredibly dangerous."

"I understand, Captain. Keep us informed about your progress and we will continue to focus on defensive strategies in the meantime."

Marlena was glad that her commanders were sensitive to her situation. She knew none of them would make plans for a counterattack against the UEDF until both of her children were safe. Not that anyone in the ICC was eager to go to war against Earth, only that they all knew it was just a matter of time until Earth ran out of resources and Harruhama would attempt to seize the colonies, by any means necessary.

"Captain Velez, please inform Captain Mercer what you told me before she arrived," Commander Watson said.

"Thank you, Commander. Good to see you alive and well, Mrs. Mercer," Velez said delightedly.

"Good to see you the same, Armando," Marlena smiled.

The two had become acquainted during the voyage between Earth and Aeris VII. After the incident of 2115, Captain Velez and his wife were so appreciative of her rescuing them, they had been instrumental in electing Marlena as leader of the ICC.

"I received a report two weeks ago from the Dytopa II Colony in the Omega Nebula. Apparently a man named Dr. Arminus has discovered a very large metallic object in the ground near the city of Tiberius Falls," Velez said, the sense of excitement evident in his voice.

"What is it?" Marlena asked eagerly.

"They have no idea, but the low-altitude, monster storms on that planet made it impossible to investigate until they clear up. It could take months. I will send you the reports as I receive them."

"Monster storms?" Marlena inquired, "Are they that bad?"

"It is my understanding that it is a literal term. The report of the wildlife on Dytopa reads like the stuff of nightmares," Velez stated with a shutter.

"Forward me the report on the structure and the wildlife report," she began. "I'll try not to read it too close to bedtime."

The ICC commanders shared a chuckle despite themselves.

"If that's all, Captains?" Commander Watson asked after a moment. "Representative Gellar, your item?"

"Thank you, Commander, and welcome back to Aeris, Captain Mercer. Congratulations on the retrieval of your son. I look forward to meeting him the next time you come to Sapphire," Brenda Gellar began sincerely.

Marlena wasn't watching the console just then, but she could tell by her tone that Representative Gellar was smiling.

"Thank you, Brenda."

"I also wanted to express my condolences for the loss of your husband. We received word two weeks ago about his passing. I am deeply sorry, from the way you spoke of him he sounded like a great man."

"He was. Thank you for saying so," Marlena said quietly, the edge of pain evident in her voice.

"Moving on to business; we have intercepted encrypted long-range messages from Sapphire's internal network. Someone has been accessing our data and transmitting information. We assume that the EMC has a spy, probably more than one snooping around our systems. We have been unable, thus far, to break the encryption, but I wanted you all to be aware of it."

"A good spy wouldn't make a mistake like that," Marlena remarked insightfully. "I would assume that it's a ruse to keep our focus on the network security instead of something else."

"Why would a spy even alert us to his presence then?"

"Perhaps it's to test our awareness, preparedness, or response. I strongly recommend giving the EMC agent as little data as possible and perform any investigations covertly."

"That is why you're our leader, Marlena," Representative Gellar said, sincerely.

"Is there any other business?" Commander Watson cut in.

Commander Watson went down the list, making sure each member of the ICC had a chance to include any parting remarks. Hearing none, he adjourned the meeting, leaving Marlena alone with her thoughts.

The idea of a spy reporting back to Earth troubled her, especially considering how spread out her fleets were. Unable to act immediately on it, however, she went back to reading the reports on her table, finding that she was very curious about just what a "monster storm" entailed.

⁓

The trip by boat to the shore only took Alex about ten minutes once he got up to speed. He'd found an open dock, secured his lines and disembarked.

Sapphire City was nothing like Alex expected it to be. Every building was designed with a similar architectural theme: the maximum efficiency of the materials used to produce them. Every structure was like an art work designed to create a sense of wonder that such a thing was possible. There was not a superfluous archway or column; no flare for its own sake.

Even the houses that dotted the shore of the lake were built with this theme in mind. Alex couldn't find one home that had an unnecessary feature in its design. Back on Earth, when they would drive anywhere, William would always show Connor and Alex what he meant by "the integrity of a building" when he would show them numerous little window shutters on homes that were there just for looks. He called it "lazy superfluous architecture" and was all too happy to point out that those shutters were unnecessary in their climate, didn't close, and even if they could close, would only cover about half the window.

Alex could see a lot of his stepfather's vision in the structures that surrounded him. The thought that the man hadn't survived to see his vision manifested in an entire city made Alex wince. He shook the thought away, letting himself relax and take in the city.

The streets were bustling with activity, people walking and driving small, three-wheeled vehicles that were enclosed with a bubble-like dome. It occurred to him that the only roads on Aeris were inside the city and small highways that led to other nearby towns and mining communities, so the need for larger street vehicles was almost non-existent. He had seen heavier mining vehicles flying low over the lake on his way in and realized that these streets would never see the heavy tires of a semi-truck.

A paper flyer fluttered down the street before getting caught on a lamp-post, capturing Alex's attention. He noted how out of place the page was on otherwise clean streets. A well-dressed man took a few steps out of his way to collect the garbage and deposit it in a bin, smiling the entire time. Most of the people Alex had seen in Sapphire City smiled, as if they truly enjoyed their lives. For someone who had grown up under the harsh rule of the UEDF, Alex saw a profound contrast between the citizens of both cultures. Where on Earth there was an aura of desperation and dread, on Aeris there was joy.

He proceeded into a nearby cafe and sat down at a table near the window, offering him a view of the street and the harbor beyond. A young woman, who couldn't have been more than a year or two older than Alex, came to take his order. She was pretty. Her long, blonde hair swayed as she walked, causing Alex to stare. She had bright-green eyes that caught the light in a way that made them dance as she smiled. A smile that gave Alex butterflies in his chest when he inhaled.

"What can I get for you, hon?" she asked softly, sweetly.

"What do you have that's good here?" Alex managed to stammer.

"Everything is good! But I'll get you a menu," she replied with a wink.

She turned to walk away, Alex's eyes following her every step. She walked like a girl who was happy to be alive, each step graceful and with purpose.

"Here you go," she said, handing him the menu.

"Can I ask you something?" He smiled up at the pretty girl.

"Sure, hon." She matched his smile.

"What is it about this place? Everyone seems so happy here."

"That's easy. We're free! Every day we wake up we know that we exist for the sake of our own happiness, so we do."

The concept seemed simple enough, a society of free people living by their own rules, away from the intrusive hands of the UEDF. Alex suddenly realized why his mom had fought so hard to keep the UEDF out of this place.

"You're not from around here, are you? What colony did you come from?" she asked casually, sitting down in the booth across from Alex.

"I'm from Earth. The only other colony I've been to was Atmos XI, and was only there for a day."

"Atmos … That means you're Captain Pereira, right? I heard about what you did there; you saved a lot of people."

"Yeah, I guess so. I'm Alex."

"Lyria Shepherd, owner of the Cerulean Sky Café," she said with a smile, standing up to bow with a slight flourish.

"You own this place? You can't be more than seventeen!" Alex said with disbelief.

"Back at ya! I don't think most people would think a guy your age was a war hero, do you?"

"I suppose not," Alex said wistfully as the weight of his actions settled upon his shoulders.

Alex knew that what he did to help his mom and the colony of Atmos XI was right, but doing so meant turning on his squadron, his friends and Earth. Just then, Alex wasn't sure "hero" was a titled he deserved.

"I'll give you a minute to look over that menu. Call me over when you're ready," she said sensing his hesitation.

Alex watched Lyria walk behind the counter and pour a cup of coffee for the only other patron in the café. The man was reading a book quietly and seemed comfortable on the stool at the counter where he sat.

The Cerulean Sky was a fitting name for the place; large, open windows looked out onto the harbor on one side, and out toward the mountains on the other. The rolled glass allowed a lot of light in and a good view of the cloudy skies above. The walls were painted a light blue, with a mural behind the counter of a lion running in a field on a sunny day.

It was cozy and made Alex comfortable. He felt like he could sit there all day staring out at the wonders of Aeris VII. Looking at the menu, he decided on something called "Baldur's Banquet," which, by the description, sounded to Alex like a cheesesteak sandwich.

"Lyria," Alex asked as he was ordering, "what's with the names of your sandwiches?"

"It's just for fun, Alex." Her melodic voice practically sang his name as she skipped off to the kitchen to prepare his food.

Alex found himself smiling, genuinely enjoying his day in Sapphire City, the heavy thoughts of war diminished in his mind. When Lyria brought out his sandwich, she sat with him at the table while he ate. They talked a little and smiled at each other a lot. She told him about life in the city and asked him about his life in the military. When he was finished, Alex paid his bill with some silver coins his mom had given him.

"I'm going to be in town for a while before I go back home; what are you doing after work?" Alex asked, hoping his words didn't sound too eager.

"I'm going to hit my lunch rush here in about an hour and will close up when everyone leaves after another two. If you want to come by in three hours or so, we can go for a walk by the lake?"

"I'll see you then," Alex said, both he and Lyria wearing big smiles.

The rest of the day Alex wandered the small city, stopping at art galleries and hobby shops. He noticed a lot of artwork in the galleries were similar to the ones William had bought for the front drive of their house; men carving themselves out of stone, women running in pure delight, and even dancers swirling, grasping to one another. Everything about the way Sapphire was built seemed purposeful in a way that made him miss his stepfather.

"I think I get it," Alex whispered to himself.

He walked to the park near the dock and found a place to sit, letting the hours pass thinking about other things William had told him during his childhood. He had been lost in memories when an alert on his OMBI reminded Alex of the time. A smile grew on his face as he made his way back toward the Cerulean Sky where he found Lyria closing up for the day.

"You're back!" she stated gleefully.

"I'm back," Alex replied, suddenly unsure of himself.

After a few awkward moments, Lyria smiled and took Alex's hand, leading him toward the lake.

"Where were you from? On Earth, I mean." Alex asked as they walked.

"Seattle. I lived there with my aunt after my parents passed," Lyria explained.

"Oh, I'm sorry," Alex offered.

"Thank you. I was really young when it happened, and I don't remembered much about them. Even Earth seems so long ago, that most of my memories are of pictures I have, rather than actual places I've seen," she said quietly.

The breeze off of Lake Amsvartnir felt good to Alex as they

walked. Much of the lakefront near the city was paved with a walking trail, which followed the water's edge. Few other people were out and other than occasional courteous greetings, they were mostly left alone.

"I'm from Healdsburg," Alex began.

"I know. Everyone knows the story of your family. Your mom is pretty famous, there wouldn't be an Aeris VII without her," Lyria replied with reverence in her voice. "I was really sorry to hear about your stepdad."

Alex swallowed back a wave of grief.

"I'm sorry, I shouldn't have…" Lyria said seeing Alex wince.

"It's okay. Thank you for saying so. It's been hard getting over the idea that he's gone. I really miss him," Alex said, stopping to look out over the lake.

They stood quietly together until dusk, letting the somber mood fade away like the setting sun. They walked back, holding hands, until they reached the door of Lyria's apartment.

"Will you come back to town soon?" she asked, the edge of hope in her voice.

"It only takes me about ten minutes by boat, so I should be able to come back fairly often," Alex replied, wearing a smile on his handsome face.

"Well, you know where I'll be. You can message me too." Lyria wrote down her contact information and handed it to Alex.

The two smiled at each other, neither walking away.

"Goodnight, Miss Shepherd" Alex finally said, kissing the girl's hand softly.

"Goodnight, Captain Pereira," Lyria replied in a whisper, saluting as she smiled.

The walk back to the boat was full of hope and smiles. Alex hadn't been sure what to expect when he'd come to town that day, but he was feeling truly happy for the first time in months.

With night falling, Alex activated the *infrared* option on his OMBI and began the short nautical trek back home.

⌒

Alex wasn't the only one in Sapphire City smiling that night. A plain-faced man dressed in bland clothing that concealed mechanized battle armor, was watching him from the docks as he sped away on his boat. He had recognized the boy as one of his secondary targets earlier that day when he spotted him walking in town.

Using the enhanced vision of his ocular implants, the EMC operative followed the boat's progress toward the small island, where he was sure he would find his primary target.

CHAPTER 5

The best laid plans of mice and men

W HEN CONNOR WALKED INTO THE BLUE ARMY common area, the room went silent. Everyone in the Ombicademy knew he had been transferred to Green Army, and were all glad he hadn't been allowed to battle for the last three months. No one was sure why, but the soldiers of Blue Army had received threatening messages on their OMBI mail applications to avoid speaking to the former commander of the class of 2126. The message had said he was dangerous and that "immediate and severe" punishment would befall anyone who talked to him.

Connor took a deep breath, not feeling good about his return to the Blue Army barracks at all. He'd been aware that the members of his original army hadn't been allowed to speak with him. Soon after getting snubbed in the hallway, Connor had used his OMBI to figure out why. Using his own name as a keyword, he searched the entire database of mail in the Ombicademy, learning about the Head Commander's edict. He wasn't interested in the other messages as much, mostly speculation among soldiers about why Connor had suddenly become a danger.

"Well, I guess I should start," Connor said uncomfortably.

The faces of four classes of Blue Army soldiers stared back at him, unsure of what to expect.

"I got a message that my brother had gone on a mission in the Eagle Nebula that wiped out his entire squadron, so I stole a ship and went to see for myself. I guess the EMC frowns on kids stealing experimental spacecraft from them."

No one said anything.

"So, after a talk with the Head Commander, he decided he was ready to let me come back to Blue Army … so here I am!" Connor finished.

Toby "Manzar" Jenkins got up from his table in the back of the common room and began walking toward Connor. He'd been one of Connor's friends and a squad leader under Connor's command. The blond-haired kid walked straight up to him, staring at his face thoughtfully. The room remained quiet.

"You stole a ship and flew it to the Eagle Nebula?" Manzar said with disbelief.

"Yeah, that's the story."

"That's AWESOME!" Manzar shouted.

The room erupted with laughter while Connor's old friends ran to see him. Then a barrage of questions began…

"What was Green Army like?" One kid shouted.

"Why did they seal the training rooms?"

"What is space like?"

"How did you get the Head Commander to let you back?"

Connor couldn't keep up with who was asking what, but after a moment the commotion died down. It was almost like he'd never left and, surrounded by his friends, Connor felt a sense of levity. The reunion went on for several minutes before Marshall "Ladder" Wade spoke up.

"You know we all got threatening letters about speaking with you. I wanted to, but I didn't want to get in trouble." Shame filled the tall, skinny boy's voice.

"Nothing to worry about, I would have done the same thing," Connor offered, trying to make his friend feel better.

"No, you wouldn't have," Aaron "Carl" Michaels chimed in. Carl was one of the strongest kids in Blue Army and he knew Connor's temperament well, having once been sent to the infirmary after a regrettable incident where he had tried to betray his former commander. "You would've sent back a message telling the Head Commander where he could shove his threat."

"Well, yeah probably," Connor said with an admitting grin.

"Can you forgive us?" Carl asked, smiling at Connor hopefully.

"I've forgiven worse." Connor matched Carl's grin. "I wouldn't want you guys to get in trouble for me. But speaking of that letter…"

Connor activated his OMBI and began typing quickly, grinning to himself as he typed furiously on the virtual keypad. After a minute he was done and everyone's OMBI in the room lit up.

"To: Blue Army Soldiers

Subject: Connor Pereira

Message: Connor is awesome and I suck. You can talk to him again. I won't ever stop being an idiot though, so ignore future messages from me.—Colonel Setzer (Head Commander)"

The kids in Blue Army burst out laughing at Connor's prank.

"How did y'all do that?" Wade "Hunter" Winchester asked in his deep Texan accent.

"A trick I picked up while I was killing time. They wouldn't let me train or battle, so I had to do something. I decided to hack the Ombicademy networks," Connor said with a mischievous grin.

"How?!" Hunter replied excitedly.

"I actually don't really know. My OMBI sort of helped me figure it out. Like when I used to train with Omega, only on the little screen." He held his left arm out in front of him.

"Well, be careful with that. You don't want to get thrown out of here," Marcus "Flayer" Ramirez said, walking up behind Connor. The dark-haired boy was the commander of Blue Army class of 2123 and had been at odds with Connor when he first arrived.

"Hey, Flayer, did you ever figure out how to get into the training room?" Connor asked the older boy.

"I did, but like, a week later they welded them all shut." Frustration filled Flayer's reply.

"Oh, about that; I got the Head Commander to let us all train again. He wants it supervised, but at least we can work on some stuff."

"Really? That's awesome! Maybe we can see how 2126 does against 2123, eh?" Flayer said, grinning.

"That would be fun. Let's do that sometime soon," Connor said, excited about the idea of training with older kids.

The rest of the reunion was an exchange of stories and reminiscing of fun battles. Clearly his friends had missed him as much as he had missed them; everyone except Cat. Amanda "Cat" McTaggart had been Connor's first friend in the Ombicademy, he even thought at one point she might be his girlfriend the way she would hold his hand when they talked. She hadn't come over to join in the celebration of Connor's return to Blue Army. Instead she sat back on her chair, watching him quietly. When he waved at her from across the room, she looked away.

Connor looked at Carl for an explanation, but the kid just shrugged at him and grimaced as a reply.

Connor learned that his friend Liam "Skulls" Butler had been appointed as the commander of Blue Army after Connor was removed from the school. Under the leadership of Liam, Blue Army hadn't done well. He wasn't a bad squad leader and took orders well. It was clear, though, that he lacked the confidence to give orders and trust his mind to work out problems quickly.

He had even stayed in his original bunk, leaving the commander's bed open.

Connor agreed to talk with him about it and, now that the training rooms were open, work on some tactics to help him improve. Connor held no illusion that the Head Commander would give him command of Blue Army again, so he decided to make that best of it and help his friends do the best they could.

At the end of the day, Connor threw himself on his old bed, exhausted. It felt like he had never left in a way, except when he would look across the room at Cat, she didn't smile at him like she used to, but would only look off in the opposite direction.

He didn't understand, but he resolved to work it out with her as soon as he could.

—

On the opposite side of the Ombicademy in the Red Army barracks, Johnny "Mouse" Perez sat plotting with his squad leaders. He had been Connor's friend before they joined the Ombicademy. Two days after Connor received his draft notice, Johnny's father had enlisted him into the UEDF, telling him that it would build character.

After being put in separate armies, Johnny and Connor had become rivals. Johnny found himself hating Connor for his success in the Ombicademy and was glad when he heard about the Green Army transfer. When he found out that somehow Connor had talked the Head Commander into letting him back into Blue Army and into the training rooms, Johnny was livid.

"I don't know how we're ever going to beat them while he's on their team," he began with his commanders, sitting on the floor in the Red Army barracks. "Even though he's been out for three months, I still think he has more points than me. I have only gotten like four thousand the whole time!"

It was all rhetoric they had heard before. The squad leaders of Red Army 2126 were getting used to Johnny's tirades about how unfair it was that he didn't have more than someone else, especially Connor.

"Well, I think we had our shot. We had four armies and he beat us," George "Hammer" Brink said slowly.

For a kid who was supposed to be among the brightest kids in the world, Hammer was not exactly sharp; none of them were. As a commander, Johnny had always thought it was better that his squad leaders were slower than he was, so he had picked the three slowest kids in Red Army.

"That's what I am saying. He had so many points he summoned a giant robot that wiped Green and Yellow out of the fight!"

"We still had Black Army with us and they are really strong," Russell "Snake" Faulkner said quietly. Russell spoke like someone who didn't intend to be heard.

"Yeah, they're a problem too; Black Army got a lot better troops than we did. It seems like all the other armies got better soldiers," Johnny whined, slamming his fist into the ground.

"Yeah, all my squad does is run in and get beat up. They aren't even very good at fighting! We need some help; maybe we should go to the training rooms too!" Mikey "Rat" Jenner chipped in. Of all his squad commanders, Johnny liked Rat the least. He had a cooler call sign for one, but he also always came up with a lot of ideas and Johnny found that obnoxious.

"Don't be an idiot, Rat! We shouldn't have to do extra work to be as good as they start out! We have to think of a good plan to take Connor out, or else every time we charge in we are going to get beat."

"How about we beat him up," Hammer said simply.

The four leaders of Red Army smiled at each other.

"I heard that, in the training room, you can get stunned.

Maybe we can shoot him a few times to stun him, and then beat him up," Rat cut in.

"That's an even better idea. Let's see if we can get the Head Commander to schedule a training day for us and Connor."

Their plan set, the leaders of Red Army went back to lying on their bunks, waiting for class to begin.

—

In a high orbit around Mars, the white hull of the Station Sigma absorbed the light of the sun, casting a tiny shadow on the red planet below. Inside the thick walls of the battle station's war room, an older man with a deep scar over one eye was reading a report about station supplies. For years, Colonel Lemmon had served as the commanding officer of both the Station's garrison, as well as four hundred OMBI-Enhanced students without any problem receiving supplies from Earth.

He read the report with disbelief that medical supplies were to be rationed and servings of food were to be reduced by twenty percent per soldier until further notice. Colonel Lemmon never thought he would see the day when a critical military installation would have to undergo rationing for basic supplies. His mind wandered to the front lines of the war he still believed was being fought over the colonies, and the thought made the Colonel feel like he was helpless.

When he finished the report, Colonel Lemmon read his next set of orders. The two still-active members of Black Squadron were to be issued new orders. He had gotten to know both boys over the year that they had been training on the station, along with the other thirty-eight members of the squadron, and was saddened to hear about the massacre of the Eagle Nebula.

Philip "Vector" Wick was a heavyset, obnoxious kid who had always been concerned about the competitive aspects of

OMBI training. He was more worried about getting points than working with his squad and, as a result, was not very popular among his teammates. He had injured himself during the removal of his second inhibitor chip, the device that kept OMBI manifestations virtual, when he manifested a sword that punctured his leg.

The other boy was Austin "Vertigo" Hughes.

"I am sorry to hear about the loss of your friend, Austin," Colonel Lemmon began, addressing one of Ombicademy's best students. Austin was the kind of boy who followed orders to a fault, a true believer in the mission of the UEDF. "I know you and Alex were close and I know it must be hard on you."

"Thank you, sir," Austin replied impassively. A lean boy and extraordinary fighter, Vertigo would have commanded Black Army in the Ombicademy if he would have had a stronger grasp of group tactics and been able to keep up a higher kill/death ratio than Alex had. At one point, he even had more kills than Alex, but he had earned an early second death and Alex's otherwise perfect ratio kept him in charge.

"Now that you both have recovered from your respective wounds, I have new orders for you," Lemmon continued, unsure of what to make of Austin's emotionless response.

"Vector."

"Yes, sir," Vector said proudly.

"You are to return to the Ombicademy to supervise training of the students until further notice."

"WHAT? Sir, I can fight Gortha now, why should I go back to train the little lizard babies?"

"Stow that, Private. These are your orders and I expect you to follow them. Training our personnel is every bit as important as fighting on the front lines."

"Yes, sir," Vector said, sounding uninspired.

Colonel Lemmon stared at Vector for a long time, wondering

why the new Head Commander of the Ombicademy would have sent a request for the kid.

"Dismissed, Vector," Lemmon said, wanting him to be gone as soon as possible.

When the room was clear, Lemmon continued.

"Austin, the EMC has ordered me to release you to them to undergo specialized training as an operative."

Austin's eyes widened as he spoke. "Operative, sir? I thought they were made up to scare citizens."

"Evidently not, Corporal; you are one of the best soldiers I have had the pleasure of training. There is a shuttle leaving at 1300 that you need to be on. Good luck."

With that, Austin saluted his former CO and shook his hand.

Alone in the war room, Colonel Lemmon went back to the reports he had been reading about supply deficiencies, wondering how he was going to enforce a twenty percent reduction in food portions.

CHAPTER 6

Sparks on wet grass

C LARION WAS A SMALL TOWN IN THE MIDDLE OF A VERY large corn field. The people who lived in that part of Iowa were mostly farmers who lived unexciting, ordinary lives untouched by the UEDF except during the biannual tax evaluation. Farmland had been increasing in value with the food shortages occurring around the world, so when the UEDF built a political detention camp in the middle of fifty acres of corn, the citizens of Clarion were upset. They organized and each wrote a strongly-worded letter to their UEDF Representative, Councilman Stahl, but after two months of waiting, they heard nothing back.

The camp was built out of low-end portable buildings mixed in with some large tenting in the middle of a graded-out, dirt field. The facility was surrounded by three rows of large razor-wire fences with two tall guard towers at the corners, which had one guard each.

Corporal Stanley Weiss had been assigned to the facility the day before and still didn't know the names of any of the men in his unit. As he left the barracks on that hot, July morning he only half-heartedly returned the salute from the guard at the gate as he entered the compound with the prisoner list.

"How are they today, Private?" Weiss asked reading down the list.

"The prisoners, sir?" The guard seemed perplexed.

Weiss nodded expectantly.

"Fine? I guess, Sir," The guard stammered. It was obvious that he had never been inside the perimeter.

Looking upon the camp, the prisoners didn't seem fine. The conditions were terrible. Water for the camp came from a well with a hand pump, which was producing less water each day that the prisoners had used it. The temporary plumbing had been clogged for a couple of weeks, and sanitation was becoming a nightmare as raw sewage began running in ditches to the edge of the fence line where they abruptly stopped, leaving large muddy pools.

Food was delivered in a crate by a helicopter, which dropped it twice per day until recently, when they began delivering one, half-full crate per day. Corporal Weiss had heard about food shortages, but the 350 troops stationed in the barracks just outside of camp didn't seem to go without.

Reading the list of names, Weiss was surprised that he recognized many of them. Twenty-four small-time politicians who had been vocal opposition to the UEDF, seven news anchors who had been reporting on news that had not been approved by the UEDF censor bureau, an author who had written a book that had a UEDF officer as an antagonist, the parents of a soldier who had been drafted at the age of 10, who had apparently been angry about it and thirty-two attornies who had taken cases against UEDF employees. The remaining seemed to be a mix of hundreds of other suspicious people who, at one time or another, expressed dissatisfaction with the current regime.

Weiss had read some of the specific biographies prior to the assignment, but most of them were filled with vague, familiar accusations.

The stink of sweat and sewage permeated the air as Weiss walked through the camp. A few prisoners were awake and sitting outside, watching the new officer as he passed by. Some kind of illness was reported to be spreading, and raspy coughing broke the silence often.

Weiss hated it here already. He was beginning to understand why the soldiers never entered the perimeter. Shaking his head, he went back to the barracks to wait out the heat of the day.

The day passed uneventfully, other than the disorganized rush to the food crate, as was the daily ritual inside the fence. The unbearable heat of summer was somewhat diminished by cool evening breezes that occasionally rolled across the plains. A full moon was rising on the night of July 11th when the prisoners were awakened by the sound of a low rumbling. With not a cloud in the sky that night, confusion spread among the camp.

"Can't be thunder, can it?" one man said to no one specifically.

"Doesn't look like rain to me," another chimed in passively.

The rumbling ceased after a couple of minutes, causing the minor stir in the camp to die down. The prisoners, lying outside on the ground in the cool night air, were settling back to sleep when a bright flash caused them all to awaken.

The fireball lit up the night for miles around as the barracks that housed the 17th regiment of the UEDF International Guard exploded, sending debris and ash high into the night sky. The sound of the explosion roared through the camp soon after, the shock wave knocking many of the prisoners to the ground.

⁓

The Dragoon walked slowly around the burning wreckage, knowing there would not be any survivors. His heavy boots left deep imprints upon the ground as the man adjusted his bandana and hat to fully conceal his face.

"Might have overdone it a little," he commented to himself as he observed the destruction around him. He had raided a small arms depot in Des Moines earlier that day and had been surprised to find a cache of C4 explosives in a box near the back of the depot. He used some of it to level the depot then and used the rest on the barracks.

When he'd first approached the camp that evening, he had covertly planted the explosives around the barracks before walking up to the guard at the door and demanding to see the commander.

The man who commanded the 17th IG regiment had been rude and unpleasant. When asked to surrender, the man had actually tried to shoot the Dragoon in the chest. He took the man down quickly, and while he regretted having to destroy the entire encampment, he knew it would be difficult to convince the troops to surrender with their commander dead.

The soldiers that had been standing guard at the gates of the detention camp began running back in the direction of the smoldering barracks as debris began falling out of the sky. The area was lit by a bright fire as ash rained down like snow. A spotlight glared down from a nearby guard tower and stopped when it illuminated the outlaw's position.

"Attention, intruder, give up peacefully!" the guard in the tower said into the megaphone.

The man laughed loudly, looking up at the guard tower then back to the barracks he had just destroyed.

"Does it seem to you like there is any chance of this ending peacefully?" the Dragoon shouted up to the guard tower as he pulled the large, triple-barreled weapon off his back.

The guard in the tower fired a shot from his rifle, which flew wide. The Dragoon didn't waste any more time as he fired his modified, heavy shotgun at the tower. Tiny, explosive pellets detonated as they impacted the structure, sending it tumbling to the ground, scattering splinters and glass onto the area around it. A second barrage of explosive pellets sprayed into two guards that had been running toward him, causing them to detonate messily.

The man winced slightly at that.

The Dragoon's left hand went to an internal pocket of the leather duster he wore, grabbing two more explosive pellet shells, and loaded them quickly.

Another soldier came around from the far side of the camp, discharging his automatic rifle wildly as he ran. The Dragoon held the shotgun in his left hand and removed a large revolver from his belt with his right, taking aim at the incoming soldier.

The heavy shot from the large pistol sent the soldier flying into the nearby cornfield. The Dragoon continued toward the series of gates, using his heavy boots to kick them down at the hinges on both sides before moving to the next one. His strength, enhanced by the mechanized battle armor he wore beneath his duster, destroyed the metal hinges, causing the gates to collapse to the ground, spraying dust into the air.

When the last gate came down, he yelled out.

"They call you dissenters ... antagonists ... nuisances to be removed! They round us up, hold us captive, leave us to die while the people watch, waiting for their next free meal. The time has come to say 'no more'! The time has come to be free!" the Dragoon yelled into the night.

"Where should we go?" one man yelled back.

"Wherever the UEDF can't find you again. Listen to the seeds of dissent being sowed in these lands and lend them your voice. The UEDF has failed you and it is time to take back the world."

"But we are fugitives! Where will we find food? How far can we get?"

Apathy. The Dragoon had known that the people in America were apathetic, but he was shocked to find out how far they had fallen. So dependent upon the UEDF's handouts, even the political prisoners were unwilling to function by themselves, unwilling to fight to be free.

"And you wonder why resources are scarce on this planet … Can you do nothing?"

"We cannot fight a global government!"

"Whether you think that you can or cannot, you're right," the Dragoon quoted whimsically, "The people of Germany fought back, and they have already thrown the UEDF out of Berlin!"

"And look where it got them! They have no food or supplies anymore!" a man in a torn jacket retorted.

"If you give up, you will die here. This is not going to get better on its own!" the dragoon fired back.

"Says a terrorist! If we follow you, we are dead for sure!" the man said, followed by murmurs of agreement.

The Dragoon grimaced under the red bandana tied around his face. Accepting that his time had been wasted here, he turned to walk back out of the prison. He had gone there to make a daring rescue and lead the people to freedom, but what he'd found was the best hope America had for a revolution made apathetic by the promise of a half-full food crate.

He turned around to watch the prisoners, fearing their freedom, huddle back into their tents and portable trailers.

"Fine," he whispered quietly, walking away. "I'll do it the hard way."

He got upon the large motorcycle that he'd ridden out into the middle of the cornfield and pulled a pair of high-resolution night vision goggles out of a bag on the side. He placed them over his eyes and rode away to the south with his lights off.

⏜

Corporal Weiss had listened to the man's speech from the guard tower at the far end of the compound where he had gone earlier to clear his head. He'd hid when the barracks exploded, scared of the dangerous outlaw who attacked his regiment. He hadn't agreed with the treatment of the prisoners, thinking such conditions were no way for men to live. He wasn't even sure he disagreed with a lot of the opinions that had caused some of them to be arrested in the first place.

The lone remaining officer of the 17th IG regiment put his head down in shame; disappointed in his own cowardice and angry at himself for not feeling mad at the Dragoon. He'd heard the man's speech and watched as the political prisoners denied themselves their freedom. As he climbed out of his perch, he wasn't sure what had surprised him more, the fact that one man had annihilated his entire regiment or that of several hundred prisoners who were supposedly revolutionaries, not one was willing to stand up and follow the man who had given them freedom.

Corporal Weiss was similarly confused by his own feelings. The idea that he sympathized more with a supposed enemy more than his own commanders shocked his sense of self. Disheartened, the man dropped his weapon on the ground and walked out into the night, abandoning his post.

⏜

Two days after the incident, the media issued a statement regarding a minor event involving an accidental explosion that cost the lives of three hundred and fifty soldiers who had been monitoring a temporary processing facility.

When the camp was investigated after two days of no

contact with the 17th IG regiment, the gates were down but all of the prisoners were still there, waiting for their food crate.

—

"Councilman Stahl, you have a problem in your region. A terrorist is attempting to undermine our rule," Councilwoman Morgan said matter-of-factly over the video screen.

"Well, it's not working. Despite his efforts, we are still in control of the Clarion Detention Facility and all prisoners have been accounted for," Stahl replied, angry that he was absorbing the brunt of an argument he could not control.

"I don't understand. Why didn't any of the prisoners try to escape?" Councilman Moreau asked, sounding genuinely confused.

It was General Harruhama who explained with an uncharacteristic parable, "A farmer who wanted meat, one day left some food out, which drew many animals in. A patient man, he built a long fence and put the food out for a second day, the animals came back again and ate near the fence. On the third day he built a second fence, vertical to the first, and the animals walked around it and came to eat. The next day he built a third fence and still the animals came. Finally, on the fifth day, the man put out the food, and waited for the animals to come; when they arrived he closed a large gate behind them, caging them in. But the animals didn't mind, so long as the food kept coming."

"But what good are people who only exist for handouts?" Moreau asked, feeling very dirty for some reason he couldn't quite explain.

"Ah, my good Councilman Moreau, don't you see? If we placate a majority, even in a historically rebellious nation, they will keep themselves in check."

"Then why worry about a man trying to stir things up?" Moreau asked quietly.

"What we cannot allow is a symbol of revolution or freedom to influence the hearts and minds of those who still produce in this world. If the man inspires the ones who are held down by their fellows, then we will lose control of our resources, which are strained as it is. Councilman Stahl, this 'Dragoon' is in your region. Use whatever means necessary to bring him in, alive if possible."

"I will see to it," Stahl said, clearly unhappy that he was being stuck with the problem.

"How goes the progress of the 2nd fleet battle group in the Hourglass Nebula?" Stahl asked, trying to change the subject.

"It is proceeding on schedule. They should arrive at Aeris within two days. Our source, planet side, has informed me that all but five Battle Frigates from the 3rd and 5th fleets are on patrol in other sectors, and of those, two are grounded for maintenance. Our seven frigates should easily overwhelm them," Harruhama said confidently.

The conference ended shortly after, leaving Councilman Stahl with his staff making plans to trap a terrorist.

—

Aboard the UEDF Cortez, Captain Balvoon was making preparations for battle. He'd been going over his plans with his officers for over a week and had been refining the specifics as details from long-range sensors start coming back.

He had been informed that the early warning system on Aeris VII would be disabled by an operative stationed on the planet and that his attack would be a surprise. He had new data on the enemy force as well.

The plan would be simple, with only three enemy Battle

Frigates to contend with, he would focus his fire until all three were destroyed, sending his Anubis Squadrons down to the planet's airfield to disable or destroy the other two frigates before they could launch.

Confident in an easy win that would mean the end of the *Independents,* Captain Balvoon was smiling as his battle group neared their target.

CHAPTER 7

Sapphire Night

THE SOUND OF WATER LAPPING AT SHORE ON THE Island in Lake Amsvartnir made Marlena Mercer feel at ease as she watched her son speeding away on the boat toward Sapphire City. When he had returned from the city late in the evening a week before with a boyish grin on his face, she knew he'd met a girl. She was glad when Alex opened up to her and told her about Lyria and how excited he was to introduce them.

For a moment that night, she felt like a normal mother with a normal son living a normal life in a paradise world. And even after six years apart, she felt the impulse to tell William about Alex's new romance. Her illusion came down after the momentary lapse leaving her feeling empty.

She and Alex had spent the last week working with two new Anubis gunners who had signed up into the voluntary Aeris Militia and had shown aptitude for targeting. The training went well and Marlena had been amazed at Alex's patience and skill as a teacher. As much as she hated everything that the Ombicademy represented, she had to admit that they produced a peerless soldier.

When she had asked Alex how he learned to be so patient, he just shrugged and said, "Six years of training little lizard babies, I guess." They both laughed, even though he had to explain the slang to his mom. The woman hadn't smiled much since she had been betrayed by the UEDF in 2115. Especially when she knew that she could never return home if she wanted her husband and children to have any chance at surviving. She had played dead to protect them, and though it pained her deeply, she had not regretted it for even a moment.

A month with her son had reminded her how much of her life she'd lost. Thoughts like those always made her feel anxious, especially since she still had a ten-year-old son living under the oppressive reign of the EMC.

So, on a sunny Aeris day, Marlena boarded *Tizona*, leaving a note for Alex, and went off to find a mountain to climb.

—

When he arrived at the dock, Alex deftly tied up his boat and walked straight to the Cerulean Sky Café. He was enjoying the beautiful, cool weather as he crossed the small street and walked through the door.

He was greeted with a big smile as Lyria skipped over to him from behind the counter. She hugged him tight, holding on just long enough for Alex to catch the scent of strawberry in her hair. They shared a smile and then both began to blush, realizing that the patrons of the café were all watching them.

"Ahem. So, Captain, just one today?" Lyria said awkwardly.

"Yeah," Alex replied coolly, still blushing.

"Is the counter okay?"

"Yeah, it's fine."

Alex sat down as Lyria went about her work. He hadn't seen her since they met a week before, getting caught up with training. He had thought about her a lot since then, but was still surprised by how pretty she looked in person.

"I'm sorry I haven't been back in a week," Alex began sheepishly. "I had to train some new Anubis gunners."

"It's no problem; I'm just glad you found the time," she replied playfully.

They shared another lingering smile before Lyria skipped off into the kitchen. Alex was amazed as he watched her walk out of the room. Her light-blonde hair seemed to bounce and sway with every step.

Alex knew that he was in trouble. He'd never really had a crush before. He had friends who were girls at the Ombicademy, but none of them were as intoxicating as this one.

He tried to remember what the boys at the Ombicademy had said when they had crushes on girls. But that line of thinking inevitably led him back to the day he had to turn on his squadron. He still wasn't sure how to cope with it, but he knew that it wasn't his fault. It was the fault of the UEDF and the inhibitor chips.

Alex unconsciously rubbed his OMBI, thinking about the inhibitors. He still had his 3rd inhibitor in, but he didn't really know what to expect if he removed it. The device on his wrist allowed him to operate any vehicle, command any robotic device, and materialize weapons from nowhere. He could alter his vision into any spectrum of light, detect motion, and even create force fields with a mere thought. It made him stronger and faster in ways that training alone could never match. He had trained with it for almost six whole years and it now felt like an extension of himself. The "311 Anti-Fire and Medical Robot" (AFMR), which had removed his 4th inhibitor, had told him that the 3rd inhibitor restricts the transfer of data between the wearer and the device. Currently he could manifest almost anything he could think of; what would the experience be like if the OMBI were to communicate back with him?

The thought troubled Alex while he sat in the café. He was so deep in thought that he didn't hear Lyria ask him what he wanted at first.

"You okay, Alex?" she asked, finally getting his attention.

"Yeah, sorry; I was just thinking about something," he replied, shaking away the troubling thoughts.

Alex ordered the Baldur's Banquet again, having enjoyed it tremendously the last time. After a while the room began to empty out, and Alex realized that he probably had arrived during the lunch rush. When they were alone, Alex finally spoke.

"Sorry if you were busy when I got here," He offered.

"Think nothing of it. Honestly, ever since I met you, my heart has skipped a beat every time that door opened."

Alex was smiling. "I think I know what you mean."

Lyria returned Alex's smile and the two sat staring at each other for several minutes before they realized they'd been sitting silently for some time.

"You're going to be trouble, aren't you?" A wistful smile spread across Lyria's red lips.

"Funny, I was just thinking the same thing," Alex replied in kind.

Lyria closed up the Cerulean Sky while Alex helped wipe down the counters. The two left together, walking down the street holding hands while they talked. Lyria led Alex to a part of the city he hadn't been to on his last trip, where a man was playing a guitar and singing in an outdoor amphitheater. The man was pretty good and the two sat down on the grass and listened, Lyria leaning into Alex slightly.

"A lot of people here are into the arts; they come out here to perform all the time. Do you play anything?" Lyria asked.

"Not really," Alex said with a laugh. "I used to play the drums a long time ago."

"Were you good?"

"I was pretty good. No drums at the Ombicademy though, so it's been a long time. What about you, Lyria?" Alex liked saying her name.

"No instruments. Not very well anyway, but I can sing."

"I would love to hear you," Alex said with a hint of anticipation in his voice.

Lyria smiled and stared at him for a few seconds, causing Alex to wonder just what she was seeing in his eyes. In one fluid motion she stood up and began to walk down to the stage. The man who had been playing guitar, seeing someone else approach, stood back and smiled. They exchanged a few quiet words that Alex couldn't make out from the back of the amphitheater before the man began playing a haunting melody while Lyria took center stage.

A look of focus came over her as the melodic voice of Lyria Shepherd echoed through the amphitheater.

Her eyes are the moon, in the darkest night
The stars above that guide my weary sight
She's the sunrise each morning, upon my open road
The horizon that calls me, though heavy my load
She's fair wind in my sails on quiet days at sea
The lighthouse fire burning, reaching out to me
She's the muse behind my pen, in every word I write
The spark of flames in my heart that makes my world bright
Where the wind will take me, I have not a clue
But every road I travel, leads back to you.

Alex was entranced. He watched the lithe girl swaying to the song with her eyes closed, singing sweetly with the voice of an angel. His skin was covered in goose bumps as she continued the song.

I knew her soul when we touched; knew it lifetimes past
Felt it when I held her, that this love would be my last
No matter how far in the night these wheels let me roam
My heart will be with her because her heart is my home
Where the wind will take me, I have not a clue
But every road I travel, leads back to you.

The roar of applause shook Alex from his trance. He hadn't realized that a crowd had formed to hear Lyria sing. She was smiling with tears in her eyes as she walked off the stage.

Alex got up and rushed forward through the crowd to meet her, surprised to find tears in his own eyes as well. The song had touched him and the way the girl had sung it left him sputtering for the right words.

"That was beautiful," he managed to say.

"Thank you," she replied with a smile, tears still in her eyes.

"I have never heard that before; who wrote it?"

She never got the chance to answer; a loud siren pierced the evening, destroying the moment. The audience in the amphitheater was stunned, looking at each other with panic in their faces.

"What's going on?" Alex shouted above the commotion.

A voice sounded over a loudspeaker nearby.

"Attention residents of Sapphire City, proceed immediately to the nearest shelter. Aeris VII is under attack."

———

Alex grabbed Lyria by the hand and led her at a run, following the illuminated signs that were pointing the way to the shelter. He looked up as the UEDF Anubis Squadrons flew over Sapphire City toward the airfield on the east side.

"How far is it to the shelter?" Alex yelled out over the sound of people screaming, sirens blaring and spacecrafts above.

"It's right around the corner from my house! What's happening?" Lyria screamed back, her voice on the edge of panic.

"Calm down, I'll get you there." Alex's reply was steady, calming.

She seemed to relax a bit while they ran back down the crowded streets of Sapphire City. Alex could hear explosions near the airfield when he and Lyria rounded the corner. A large holographic arrow was pointing toward a stairway that led under the buildings of the city. When they arrived, Alex turned toward the docks.

"Don't go out there!" Lyria pleaded.

"You'll be fine in the shelter. I need to get to my ship." Alex said as his eyes scanned the sky above.

The bright lights of explosions appeared in the darkening sky above Sapphire City. UEDF fighters flew above like flocks of birds, while the Aeris Militia fighters attempted to hold them back. With the night falling and the two moons of Aeris VII bright in the sky, Alex could see the tiny explosions of a battle in orbit as well.

Alex turned back to Lyria, who was clearly terrified. He pulled her in close, looking into her eyes. He could feel her heart pounding in her chest as it pressed against his. In the cacophony of the war, Alex Pereira and Lyria Shepherd shared their first kiss.

—

Alex ran as fast as he could toward the dock, putting the girl out of his mind and focusing on the larger issue ahead. Even with OMBI enhanced agility, he felt like he was taking too long. The planetary defenses were clearly being overwhelmed, and he knew he had to launch *Skoll* as quickly as he could. In his sprint, he almost missed the light flashing off the metal object out of the corner of his eye.

The long blade cut in front of Alex as he threw himself sideways into a roll. He came up with twin black scimitars already in his hands, manifested from his OMBI.

His attacker wore plain clothing and had a very common-looking face, which wore a slight grin. There was nothing about the man that made him stand out to Alex, except the fact he was holding a long sword in one hand and a gun in the other.

"Impressive, Son of Phoenix," the operative said menacingly.

"Who are you?" Alex demanded as he circled the man like a hunter stalking his prey.

"Operative One," the man replied casually, as if his name meant nothing.

Alex had heard of the operatives before. They were supposedly the assassins of the EMC, highly trained for espionage and murder. They were spoken of as a way to scare people, but most people were unsure they actually existed. The idea that the top assassin of the EMC stood before him made Alex's skin crawl.

"Okay," Alex said quietly, focusing on the man in front of him.

The man moved quickly, raising the gun in his left hand and firing several shots at the boy. Alex moved quicker, reaching into his OMBI through his Neuro-Sync, bringing up a force field between himself and the man. The bullets ricocheted harmlessly off his barrier as Alex ran forward, blades spinning.

Operative One dropped his gun as Alex closed the distance, bringing his sword across in a high arc, causing Alex to slow and block the attack. He swung out again and again with cunning strikes designed to end the fight quickly. Alex turned them away deftly and countered with measured ferocity.

The man was the top assassin in the UEDF; he had been trained for decades, completed hundreds of missions, was the perfect killer, and even he was put back on his heels by the speed and intensity of this boy's charge.

Alex sliced out high and came back low, not letting up as his scimitars bounced against the operative's frantic blade. His speed was unfathomable and, as the fight progressed, he seemed to be getting faster.

The man was not out of tricks, though, and from the sleeve on his left arm he tossed several small projectiles which exploded against Alex's force shield. In the flash of light and smoke, Operative One retreated back with several quick steps, thinking he would get a reprieve from the boy's fury.

Alex came bursting through the smoke, eyes glowing red with his thermal imaging overlay. Thin black armor began appearing over the boy's body, replacing his downed force shield as he advanced. His attacks were becoming more cunning with each swing; two scimitars came in, working the assassin's blade out wide and high. Alex then sprung forward, letting his blades dissipate and manifesting a short spear from his OMBI, which he trust at the off balance assassin.

The fight raged across the park in front of the docks, over picnic tables and around trees, the boy gaining an advantage with every step. The assassin had underestimated his mark badly. He knew the boy was well-trained and enhanced with an OMBI, but he had not been prepared for how quickly he adapted to the changing conditions of the fight. With each obstacle his weapons changed form, making it like fighting a new opponent every few seconds for the operative. It became rapidly apparent that he would not be able to beat this boy in a head-on fight.

He was running out of options. He caught a break when he spun in a circle, releasing several tiny explosive pellets which detonated against Alex's armor, giving the assassin enough of a lead to run from the fight. He sprinted as fast as the cybernetic enhancements in his legs could carry him, resolving to reevaluate his target later.

The operative in full retreat, Alex turned his attention to

the battle ahead. He had wanted to give chase, but he'd already lost several precious minutes fighting off the assassin. Making a quick decision, Alex turned and ran for the boat, activating his infrared vision, hoping that he would not be too late.

—

She'd been halfway up the side of a mountain in the Grimnir range when her communicator signaled an incoming attack. Captain Marlena Mercer ran down the side of the hill with the agility of a cat back to where she had landed her ship. It took her far less time to get to the bottom and, once inside the *Tizona*, she began powering up the engines, trying to get updates from her sensors.

Closing her eyes, she listened to the chatter on the communicator while she pieced together the battle. Seven UEDF Battle Frigates had entered the system undetected and engaged the three Indepdent defensive Battle Frigates in orbit around Aeris VII. The ambush had cost Aeris one of her frigates already and the other two were sorely pressed. Three whole squadrons of Anubis fighters had begun attacking the two grounded independent frigates as well, along with the militia troops. Both battles were hopelessly one-sided without *Skoll* and *Tizona*.

When she finally got her Anubis fighter into the air, Marlena began heading back toward the city as fast as the ship would take her. Each minute that went by caused more anxiety about her son and the state of the planet she had called home for the last six years.

As she got to the edge of Lake Amsvartnir, she saw the battle raging above the city. Fortunately the enemy fighters had been focusing on military targets and had avoided, thus far, the civilian population. She could see the small boat clipping across the water, nearing her island home, and knew that her son would be joining the fight soon.

She passed over him in the water and circled around to make sure that no enemy ships were engaging him while he was vulnerable on the boat. Seeing none, she proceeded over the city to the airfield beyond. Her instruments picked up eighty-two vessels in the air, fifty-four of which were enemy. She could see one of the grounded frigates burning already and the other was being fired upon heavily.

The militia had responded quickly, but were outnumbered and outgunned. Locking on to the nearest squadron of UEDF Anubis fighters, she declared forcefully over her communicator to her allies, "Phoenix is in the fight" while launching a barrage of missiles.

"Good shooting, Mom," she heard Alex's voice over the communicator.

"Thanks, baby" she said, grinning. The fight had been going badly for Aeris, but it was about to turn around.

"Mephisto in the fight," came his declaration as she saw the Battle Armor Vessel fly past her position into a squadron of enemy fighters with a large spear. *Skoll* moved with amazing agility and Alex's control of the vessel was practically flawless. When the strange ship emerged from the other side, half of the enemy ships in the squad were falling from the sky.

"Mephisto, they need you in Orbit, we'll clean this up," she ordered now that the numbers were a little more even.

"Affirmative, Phoenix," Alex said, using her call sign for the first time.

She watched as the black samurai armor stopped mid-flight and blasted into orbit. Turning her attention on the battle, she formed up with three other ships from the Aeris Militia and started calling targets.

—

Alex knew the fight on the surface was under control, with his mom in charge of the defenses; she had been the UEDF's most highly decorated pilot, after all. As his sensors recalibrated for zero gravity, Alex watched the numbers come back on the planetary defenses. RA fighters littered the sky from both sides; three frigates were disabled and fortunately one was an enemy, making the 6:1 ratio a little less daunting for the defenders.

The remaining Aeris Frigate was maneuvering between the two disabled ships, using them as cover.

Alex didn't waste any time when he got into the fight. Reaching through the Neuro-Sync to his OMBI, he activated the highlighting function, which proceeded to identify enemy ships by encasing them with a soft red glow. One of the enemy frigates had targeted him, but after raising his force shield and armor, he flew straight through a barrage of heavy cannon fire toward the attacking ship. He had danced to this song before and knew where UEDF capital ships were vulnerable.

"No time to be merciful," Alex said quietly to himself as he flew in front of the heavily enforced walls of the Battle Frigate's bridge. He looked through the three small windows at the crew, all scrambling to get out of the way as he smashed through using a giant hammer that he manifested in *Skoll*'s hand through his OMBI.

The vacuum of space took care of the rest. Knowing that a ship without its commander and communications was almost entirely ineffective in combat, he moved to the next frigate.

—

Captain Balvoon's grin turned into a deep frown when the strange Battle Armor Vessel entered the fight, crippling two of his frigates in under a minute. The ship worked fast and it seemed like no matter how many guns they turned on it, the enemy vessel was always one step ahead.

None of his intelligence up to that point indicated anything about a ship that was possibly stronger than his entire force. He ordered all remaining vessels to close their blast shields and use their sensors to continue the fight.

Balvoon heard the pounding outside his blast shield as the strange ship went to work. He doubted for a moment that those shields would be strong enough to hold back the vessel until the pounding stopped.

The Captain of the Cortez was in mid-sigh when the officer at the communications station started screaming.

"It went where?!"

As if to punctuate the remark, Balvoon heard a strange banging sound from somewhere below his deck, followed by the sound of an explosion.

"Sir, reports from the UEDF Marion say that the enemy vessel has boarded the Cortez!"

They listened quietly as the sounds of destruction raged through the decks below.

"Well, where is it headed?" Balvoon asked, trying desperately to keep his mind focused.

"Power core, sir."

"Damn."

Balvoon knew it was over. His surprise attack had been a complete success up until that strange ship had interfered. He didn't know what it was or where it came from, but there was no way that his remaining three ships could put up a fight against it if they remained in battle.

"Order a full retreat. Eject the core. Send all available data on that ship back to command."

—

Alex watched the core eject and followed it out of the ship. The commander had been smart enough to cripple himself and spare his crew. Had Alex been able to disrupt it, they would all be dead. He watched the ship listing lazily through the darkness as the other three enemy ships began to turn in retreat. Their Ra Squadrons were returning to the docks as well, under fire from the Aeris defenders.

"Stand down, Aeris defense. They're retreating," Alex said into his com.

"Yes, sir. Standing down," replied the squadron commanders who had been in pursuit.

It had been easier than Alex had thought; the fight was all but over as Alex maneuvered *Skoll* through the debris. He used the strong hands of his ship to repair what he could on the damaged Battle Frigates in order to prevent excessive oxygen leakage.

Knowing there would be a lot of survivors from both sides, he mentally prepared himself for the task of hauling a half-dozen Battle Frigates to the planet's surface.

CHAPTER 8

Cat and Mouse

ONNOR'S DREAMS HAD BEEN DARK EVER SINCE HE HAD
returned to the Ombicademy. He wasn't too upset by
it, since he was no longer dreaming about his mom or
stepfather dying. Mostly they were about him talking with robots
or fighting other kids. However, he wasn't getting as much sleep
at night as he wanted to. Ever since joining the Ombicademy
six months prior, he hadn't slept much. But lately it was down
to three to four hours, leaving him groggy and volatile during
the day.

So when he woke up after just two hours, he was not in a
happy mood. He knew it was late and he could still feel his muscles aching from the battle they had fought with Yellow Army
earlier that day. The battle had gone well; Yellow had modified
their tactics since Connor's last battle, and no longer just hid the
entire time. It had been a "capture-the-flag" type game though,
so Blue Army didn't have to kill everybody.

Manzar had tried to give Connor back command of Blue
Army, but had not been allowed by the Head Commander.
Instead, Manzar led the army around the academy, through the
morning training rituals, and to the arena. But when they got
there, he listened to Connor make plans, and agreed to put him

back on his own "specialist squad" that he'd been using when he was the commander.

It was an awkward arrangement, since every time Manzar issued an order, every other soldier would look at Connor, who would nod before they accepted it. But Blue Army was back to form after a couple of days.

In the melee battle with Yellow Army, Connor had started by walking straight toward the enemy base, squads flanking his progress. He never stopped walking, disarming and disabling his opponents with no weapons in his hands until he had the flag. He walked back out and back to Blue Army's base like he was walking to the commissary for lunch. It had been an embarrassment to the Yellow Army commander, who complained the entire match.

That night Connor's OMBI indicated that it was still only 2300 and he wasn't sure what had woken him up. When he sat up, he felt someone sitting on his bed and almost cried out.

"Shh," the person said.

"Whose there?" Connor demanded quietly.

"Cat." Her voice was thick with an Irish accent.

"What's the matter, Amanda?"

He and Cat hadn't said anything to each other since Connor had been back at the Ombicademy.

"When you left that day, I cried for an hour. I went out into the training room to find you, but I didn't know where you went," Cat explained in a whisper.

"You could have asked Omega," Connor said, referring to the holographic training program that he ran in the training rooms in order to test his skills.

"I tried. But he didn't appear after you ran off. I searched as far as I could without getting lost. What happened to you, Connor?"

He really liked the way she said his name. Her accent always did make it sound cooler than when he said it.

"That day I ran until I collapsed, Cat. Omega led me from there to a cave and when I walked down into it, I came out in another part of the Ombicademy. A dusty place that didn't look like it had ever been used. That's where I found that ship I flew to the Eagle Nebula," Connor explained as honestly as he could, hoping to bridge the distance between himself and his friend.

"The Battle Suit you said looked like the one your brother had?"

"Yeah, that's the one. I would have come back to find you, but I was so worried about Alex. I still don't know what happened to him."

"I'm sorry I've been cold to you. I felt like you abandoned me here. I was even called into the Head Commander's office and interrogated about you."

"I'm sorry you had to go through that."

"I told him everything, Connor. I was scared; I didn't know what to do."

"He is the Head Commander; you did what you were supposed to. I tried to tell them everything too, but they didn't believe me."

"I felt like I was betraying you. It was the worst feeling ever." Cat sniffled. Connor could tell she was crying.

He got up out of his bed and put his arm around her while she cried, waiting patiently for her to calm down. When she did, Connor spoke.

"It's all right, Cat; it's over now."

"So we're okay?"

"Yeah, we're okay. I couldn't do this without you, you know. We need to be okay," Connor said, smiling in the dark room.

Cat hugged him tightly before going back to her own bunk. Connor sat back against his pillow and thought how strange it was that she was mad at him for feeling like she betrayed him. He thought he would never understand girls as long as he lived, but was glad that he and Cat could be friends again. He'd really missed her.

He eventually found sleep again that night, after thinking for a couple of hours. When he woke up the next morning his mood had brightened a little bit. And when Amanda smiled at him from across the room, his mood brightened a lot more.

—

Vector was not happy to be back at the Ombicademy after living on Station Sigma for more than a year. Not that the space station orbiting around Mars was more comfortable than the Academy, it was a matter of pride. He had graduated near the top of the class, his battle statistics were among the highest in the school, and yet here he was, training babies how to fight.

His attitude was apparent on his face when he entered the Head Commander's office in the observation lounge of the Ombicademy. He marched up to the man's desk and saluted before sitting down in one of the room's many chairs.

"Welcome back to the Ombicademy, Mr. Wick," Head Commander Setzer said with an edge of irritation in his voice.

Vector grunted in response.

"As I am sure you know, I am the new Head Commander. My name is Colonel Setzer." The bald man spoke slowly. Vector started to wonder if the man thought he was dumb.

"Yes, I figured that. So I am supposed to help you guys train some lizard babies?" Vector asked indignantly.

"Indeed. We have re-opened the training rooms; I want you to supervise some training there."

"Why do they need to be supervised? My class used them without getting hurt."

"The reasons are not important. What is important is that

you are there to make sure that the kids don't do anything they aren't supposed to."

"Fine," Vector agreed in a huff.

"That said, what are you feelings about Connor Pereira?"

"That stupid hisser? His brother was a good commander, but that kid is irritating. Ever since they cheated on the first day I haven't been sleeping right." Vector's disdain was written all over his face.

The Head Commander smiled.

"I have received a request from the leadership of Red Army 2126 that they want to have a training session with him. I want him to explain to them how he is able to give himself tests."

"Wait, that kid gave himself tests? How?" Vector asked, sounding sincerely impressed.

"If I knew that, Mr. Wick, I wouldn't be asking you to find out," Colonel Setzer replied dryly.

"Right. Okay, well I'll get on it!"

The smile spreading on Vector's lips told the Head Commander that he was on board with the plan.

"I trust you won't interfere when they begin 'practicing.' Boys will be boys, after all."

The man's usage of air-quotes was necessary.

"Uh, yeah. I get it!"

"Good. Now get out of here, I'm busy," Setzer finished, turning his attention back to his datapad.

Vector had just began to like the man too.

—

When Connor got the message the next morning, he was in the commissary eating chocolate chip pancakes. He'd realized that the more he thought of what he wanted to eat, the more likely he would get it when he ate. He wasn't sure how he was doing it, but he was having a fun time getting only his favorite meals over and over again.

Message 1: Training Room! "You are to report to training room seven at 1100 to train with Red Army" delivered 0830 2121-07-15 From: Private Wick, Phillip (Vector)

When Connor first read it, he thought about ignoring it. He had heard someone say that they'd seen Vector back at the Ombicademy, but Connor hadn't thought much of it. The kid was an idiot, and Connor couldn't stand him. The more he thought about it though, the more he thought it would be fun to taunt him and Red Army. He wasn't sure why he had to train with a rival army, but in his foul mood, he planned on making them sorry for ever sending a message to him to begin with.

Connor found training room seven using his OMBI's return function easily enough. It was right next to the Red Army barracks. With no one waiting outside, Connor assumed that Red Army had found someone to let them in. Going to the door, Connor took a deep breath and begun to visualize himself having a good training session; no one else, though.

With a grin on his face, he entered the room.

Training room seven was different from the other rooms Connor had trained in. He came through the door into a cramped hall of what looked like a space station. Going to a nearby porthole, Connor looked down to see the planet below. He knew that the training rooms were connected somehow, but the idea of an entire virtual planet was staggering. How many other places could these rooms exit to?

Connor followed the hall down to a room that was labeled in an unfamiliar language. When he opened the door, it looked like some kind of cafeteria that had a large bay window on one side. Normally any space vehicle or station only had small windows, as they had to be thick and were seen as a weak point, structurally. This window was massive and Connor wondered what it would be like to be in space, in a virtual world. Would he freeze? Could he breathe?

His questions were interrupted when a familiar baritone voice called his name.

"Pereira!" Vector called out. He was standing next to Johnny and three other boys, all with red glowing OMBIs.

"It's 'Raptor' to you. How did you survive the battle of Eagle Nebula?" Connor asked bluntly.

"How did you know about that, hisser? I wasn't there; I got injured before the mission," Vector barked defensively.

"Lucky you," Connor quipped, looking across the room at the other boys.

"Hi, Connor," Johnny said, disdain dripping from his greeting.

"What's up, Johnny?" Connor asked, sounding sincere. They weren't friends anymore, clearly. But a part of Connor was always reminded of the simpler times of his childhood when he saw him.

"I heard about your stepfather. He was a good guy. I'm sorry," Johnny said back, surprisingly genuine.

"Whatever. You guys ready to do this or what?" Connor wasn't interested in condolences. He just wanted to get back to the point.

"Yeah, so the objective today is to teach other kids how to test themselves, so we can all acquire points faster," Vector said, emphasizing the word "points" eagerly.

"What do you mean? I activated a training program to test me. Everyone in Blue Army used it. Doesn't Red Army have their own?" Connor asked, confused.

"No! How do we use it?" Johnny asked, stepping forward. Any sympathy he may have shown before was now gone.

"Omega, can you hear me?" Connor asked to the room, looking around.

Quiet.

"I haven't used it in a long time, so maybe it doesn't work over here," Connor said with a shrug.

"Training program, activate," Vector said loudly.

Still nothing.

"Well, I don't know what to tell you guys. The only other way I found to get points outside the arena is to fight."

They could tell by the look in his eye what he meant. Connor was renowned at the Ombicademy for his hand-to-hand skills; he had completed Grand Master martial arts training within his first two months.

"Okay, kid. Let's see what you got. Red Army, get ready."

This was the plan they had developed; they wanted to teach Connor a lesson by stunning him and then kicking him while he was down. After all, "If you can't run faster, break the legs of the guy who does."

The Red Army leadership fanned out around the long dining tables in the room. The room had a lot of silver color to it. The walls were silver, and so were the tables. The serving area shone like it had never been used.

When they were ready, Connor, still standing perfectly still, yawned. "Any time you guys think you're ready."

He was surprised when the four members of Red Army drew guns and leveled them at Connor.

"Crap," Connor said to himself, diving behind a table.

Shots rang out loudly in the cafeteria. The Red Army leaders gave chase with their small hand guns, while Vector laughed from the corner.

Connor took a hit on his left arm as he dove behind another table, causing it to hang limply at his side. He felt the pain rippling through his disabled arm as he rounded the end of the low table, and ran along the outer wall of the room. Snake jumped up on a table and attempted to block Connor as he ran.

Connor spun around, leg out, sweeping the kid as he was still trying to gain his footing on the table. Snake fell hard on his back and rolled off the table and onto the floor. Seeing Vector move to block his way, Connor turned suddenly and rolled over the table on his back, taking another hit on his limp left arm, causing pain to shoot through it anew.

He landed on top of Snake and rolled over the next table, finding himself in front of Hammer. The kid, to his credit, reacted quickly, getting his gun out in front of him. Connor grabbed his wrist with his right hand and turned the kid around, using him as a shield against Rat and Mouse as they continued to fire at him.

When he got close enough, he shoved the much larger kid into Rat and then jumped up, coming down hard on both of them. Face to face with his old friend, Johnny started firing quickly, shots consistently going wide. Connor took a hit in his right arm as he came forward, leveling Johnny with a head butt to the face. Johnny went down with a cry and his nose bleeding profusely.

"Well, that isn't how it was supposed to happen," Vector laughed from across the room.

Arms stunned, Connor turned and asked, "What was supposed to happen?"

Vector shrugged. "You were supposed to go down so they could beat you up."

"Whose great idea was that?"

Realizing that he said too much, Vector closed his mouth.

"I see, you were ordered, weren't you?" Connor said, getting angry.

"Shut up, kid. You'll get me in trouble," Vector barked, coming forward.

"Well, no doubt about that." Connor retorted, taking a step toward Vector with a strange look in his eye.

"What are you doing, hisser? You want a piece of me?"

"I want the whole thing, idiot. You're bigger, stronger, and older, plus I have two arms stunned. Should almost be a fair fight," Connor taunted, eager to hurt someone.

"It's worse than you think, kid," Vector laughed, as a black shotgun manifested in his hand. It wasn't the glowing black virtual shotgun that Connor had expected, but a very real weapon that Vector was pointing at him.

"Crap," Connor said for the second time that day as he fell into a backwards roll, using his core muscles to pull himself up.

"I am not going to shoot you, kid, just hurt you a little," Vector said as the weapon changed into a large staff.

Connor didn't feel better. He turned and ran, diving over the serving table into the kitchen. Vector was on his heels, quickly swinging the large staff at him.

Connor ran into the back where the cutting tables made for a smaller corridor. As Vector came on, he changed his staff into two smaller sticks to accommodate the tighter battlefield. Connor dodged and danced out of the way, staying light on his feet, unsure of how, without arms, he could beat the larger foe that apparently got to use real weapons.

As he rolled over a table, his limp arm caught on a drawer, pulling his shoulder back painfully and stopping him midway over the table.

"Sorry, kid, but you've had it coming for a long time." Vector grinned as he swung his stick hard into Connor's trapped arm.

Connor yelped out in pain, feeling the arm snap beneath the weight of the older kid's weapon. Vector hit him again, this time across the face, causing Connor's mouth to bleed.

He was in agony. Wishing he had a hand free to fight back, he tried to get his legs under him when Vector hit him in the knee, causing him to collapse again.

He felt helpless, unable to stop this older kid from beating him. Vector was getting into the beating too, a smile growing larger on his face as he mercilessly hit Connor over and over again.

"Boys will be boys," he kept saying, until Johnny intervened. The Red Army leaders had gotten up when the stun effects wore off and walked into the kitchen as Connor fell unconscious.

"That's enough," Johnny said to Vector, while looking at Connor.

Vector stopped and looked at the other boys in the room. They stared at each other for a long while, none of them quite believing what they had just done.

They left soon after, not telling anybody that they had left a bleeding boy in the room behind them.

CHAPTER 9

To catch a Dragoon

CHESTER STAHL WAS BORN IN 2064 BEFORE THE nations merged under a one world government, before the colonies and before Earth's technology was advanced by the discovery of the ship that was now called the Ombicademy. He remembered when his father, a United States Senator at the time, told him that an alien craft was discovered in the Pacific Ocean. He had imagined what aliens would look like and what they would do if they ever came back to Earth. It was from the drawings of the ten-year-old mind of Councilman Stahl that the Gortha were created.

He was much older now and didn't often think of those days. Three failed marriages, twenty years on the Earth Military Council, and the multitude of decisions he'd made that had cost many lives left him cold inside, beyond the excited dreams of a child. Now he sat with the captains of the ten squads of the New York Special Operations unit. He had been instructed by the rest of the council to use local resources in his attempt to capture the man called "The Dragoon."

"The man is a terrorist! We need all your available units on standby," Stahl commanded, slamming his fist on the holographic map projector.

"We have counter-terrorist forces available, Councilman

Stahl," The New York Police captain offered. "But there is no way I can commit all of my officers."

At that angle, the lights from the map of New York City gave Stahl a menacing shadow across his face. He had lived through the bloodless coup six years prior when the EMC took control from the elected leadership of the UEDF and had enough of rebellions for his lifetime. He was not about to let one man turn his territory into chaos.

"Captain, I understand your position, but I assure you, there is no greater nuisance to our way of life than the Dragoon. We simply have to catch him and we cannot afford to make a mistake." There wasn't room for debate in Stahl's tone.

"On standby then. I will commit my counter-terrorist unit and ten squadrons and the rest will be waiting." The captain agreed reluctantly.

"Excellent. Now for the plan," Stahl began, bringing up the holographic map. I will announce my plans for a public speech in central park. An announcement on the Gortha War. My decoy will arrive and proceed to the podium where he will bait out the Dragoon. Your squads will be waiting in with the civilians, on rooftops here, here and here."

The captain nodded along as Stahl pointed at the various locations, admiring his quick assessments and strategy.

"Are you sure he will come? He's got to know that going after a councilman is risky." The captain asked skeptically.

"He will come. Councilmen are rarely so accessible. Kaufmann messed up by being too public with his movements and it cost him his life. The Dragoon was reported in Pennsylvania raiding supply depots, so he is close. This will work," Stahl offered confidently.

Stahl dismissed the captain and issued his press release.

The bait had been set.

—

On the holotube an hour later, advertised across the world, word of Stahl's public appearance and speech was broadcasted on every station.

The man called Dragoon was sitting in a diner outside of Harrisburg, Pennsylvania when he saw the report. Not in his western wear, the man seemed like an ordinary person, eating his lunch slowly at the counter, watching the holotube intently. While other customers slouched and complained about the weather, the government and the current excessive inflation rate, the Dragoon sat tall, absorbing it all, thinking about what it would take to push these people toward achieving their own freedom. A plan was forming in his mind, as the people on the holotube discussed the subject of planetary unity in the face of the Gortha threat.

The idea that Councilman Stahl was going to be giving a live speech the following day gave him another idea that was too good to pass up.

When the waitress brought the bill, she placed it carefully on the table, along with another slip of paper. On the paper was the girl's contact number. The man picked it up along with the bill and walked to the register where the waitress was standing. He paid with cash, tipped her, and handed her back the note.

The girl frowned as she took it back until the man held up the fingerless glove on his left hand to reveal a gold wedding band. He smiled and shrugged at the girl, who smiled back him.

"I appreciate the thought," he said sincerely.

"It's nothing. You just seemed different from any of the other guys that come through here," she said with a smile on her face.

He looked around the room for a moment and turned back to the waitress, saying, "I'll take that as a compliment."

With a slight grin, he walked out the door and got onto the

motorcycle that he'd been driving for the last few months, putting on a helmet that enhanced his vision by highlighting potential threats, which, on a motorcycle, was just about everything.

He knew he wouldn't have a lot of time to prepare and had a long way to travel, so he set to the road immediately, riding hard down Highway 78 toward New York.

—

The morning of the speech, Councilman Stahl watched the crowd form around the podium off Central Park West from the penthouse of the Dakota building. The Special Police had confiscated the penthouse from a man who had earned his riches producing high-end dramas for the holotube. He had complained at first, but eventually gave in when he realized that an EMC Councilor might feel indebted to him.

Stahl did not. Stahl believed that all property belonged to the people, and as their representative he was entitled to use it as he saw fit.

The decoy was to go on in a half hour and Stahl nervously paced the suite, anxious to see if he would be able to facilitate the public capture of the nation's top terrorist. The holotube had been downplaying the raids and attacks for the couple months of activity, on orders from the council. However, now that his capture was eminent, Stahl had the media displaying a wide range of his exploits.

This one man had been responsible for the destruction of one military prison, seven military supply depots, two national reserve banks, a holotube broadcasting hub, and a military testing facility. To say nothing of Councilman Kaufmann that he had murdered and the riot he incited in Germany. All of it was on the news that day, coming out in bits in order to make his capture more epic. Councilman Stahl had even authorized the holotube news to report on the starvation crisis in Germany as a direct result of the man's intentional destruction of supplies that were supposed to be transferred there. He hadn't destroyed any food, but the council was looking for an excuse to not send any supplies to the rioting mobs of Germany.

As the time approached for the speech, Chester Stahl sat back in his chair with a glass of bourbon, trying to relax. He knew that the ten squads of Special Police were out amongst the crowd, standing ready to take the Dragoon down, many who were disguised as civilians. Further, he had several snipers and spotters posted. As he leaned back in his chair, he felt quite confident that his plan would result in success.

—

The motorcade arrived five minutes late, pulling up to the curb near the promenade where Councilman Stahl was supposed to give his speech. Several limousines arrived and dropped off minor celebrities and holotube personalities in order to give additional hype to the coverage. The plan was for all eyes to see when the Dragoon got taken down. The crowd that gathered grew more excited when the faces of famous people appeared out of the cars.

From one, a man dressed in a black silk suit with a long coat got out to the sound of half-hearted applause from the crowd. They didn't know who he was, but they pretended all the same. When he rose his hands into the air the crowd cheered, thinking that they were supposed to. The man was smiling as he walked with a long stride toward the podium, informing the stage manager and security guard that he was to give the preliminary address to Councilman Stahl's speech. He handed a holodisc to the manager and informed him to play it when cued.

"Ladies and gentlemen, welcome! Councilman Stahl will be out to give his speech momentarily regarding the state of the

American Region of the United Earth Defense Force, along with an update on the progress of the Gortha War," the man spoke in a firm, confident voice. The crowd was silent; updates on the war were rare and always taken very seriously by the global media and the people.

"Before he begins, I would like everyone to take a moment and bow our heads for the men and women of the UEDF military who sacrificed their lives to defend us from the Gortha; we have prepared a short presentation." He cued the stage manager.

In the park the people bowed their heads reverently. Around the world, citizens watched the holotube silently as images of the original press footage of the Incident of 2115 came up to the sound of patriotic music. An image of the Andromeda appeared, which evoked an emotional outburst, causing many people to begin to cry. The image was one they had seen a lot since the event, always a reminder of the enemy lurking out in space.

The narrator began in a quiet voice, "Man's quest to colonize the galaxy, to deliver hope to the people; the Andromeda and her valiant crew seeking new resources to help sustain the human race."

The streets where quiet as the people listened, heads bowed. Everyone knew the story, and they knew what was coming next.

"Escorted by Captain Marlena Mercer, beloved mother of two, wife and defender of Earth, murdered!" The holotube showed a six-year-old picture of Marlena Mercer followed by an image of a destroyed Anubis Fighter.

"Murdered by her own government. A death ordered by the Earth Military Council in order to rally the people around their leaders against a fictitious enemy."

People in the crowd began to raise the heads, looking at each other and mumbling.

"WHAT?!"

The yell from the window eight floors up across the street

echoed out over the stunned crowd. The man who had been on stage with his head bowed like everyone else was gone in a flash. Moving with the enhanced speed of the mechanized battle suit that he wore under his clothes, he ran toward the lobby of the Dakota building.

It happened fast; the reel continued as Special Police forces emerged from the crowd and nearby streets to chase after the man into the lobby.

—

Councilman Stahl had not meant to yell out, but the shock of the best-kept secret in the EMC being publicly announced had gotten the better of him. He covered his mouth and stepped back from the window, seeing the man running with blinding speed toward the lobby of the building he was in. He quickly ordered his bodyguards to take him up to the roof and call in the emergency evacuation transport.

The video reel outside was blaring at the still-stunned crowd. A familiar image, to Stahl, came onto the screen, the face of the former Councilman Kaufmann. He was pressed against the window by a gloved hand.

"I want the truth," a man's voice demanded.

"The truth about what?" Kaufmann said, clearly afraid.

"The incident of 2115. Speak quick."

"My datapad has everything you need. Please don't kill me."

"Your datapad will be traced and you know it. You really are a clever little weasel, aren't you? Besides, I didn't follow you all the way from Berlin to read a datapad. Tell me the truth!"

"You were in Berlin? You had something to do with the riots?"

"Send the dogs in and the birds will fly. Now tell me what I want to know!"

"Okay, I will tell you everything! We were losing control of the people; we were out of resources! We had to protect ourselves, don't you understand? It was for the greater good!"

"Then it's true. The entire thing was a lie in order to seize power. The Gortha aren't real."

"It was Harruhama's idea! We had to…"

The world watched, stunned as the former councilman had the life choked out of him and then as he plunged to the streets below.

"It has all been a lie," the narrator said loudly.

Stahl was outraged as his bodyguards moved him out of the suites and down the hallway to the elevator. The six men moved with precision and speed, clearing the hall and the elevator as they all boarded.

He knew the EMC could contain the story, playing it off as terrorist propaganda. But the fact that it happened on what should have been the day that the Dragoon was to be publicly captured would cost him his life. If the man now ascending the building to get him didn't do the job, Harruhama certainly would. As the lift arrived on the large gothic roof, Councilman Stahl knew he had terribly underestimated the Dragoon's intelligence.

His bodyguards pushed him along to a flat spot as the VS91-transport shuttle hovered down to retrieve him. He looked down as he was boarding the transport, at the crowd below. They were no longer quietly listening to the broadcast, but screaming and demanding answers. He and his bodyguards aboard, the VS91-transport began to slowly pull away to the chorus of the angry shouting of the crowd. Stahl heard the people yelling out his name with disdain. He looked out to see a man in a fine silk suit with a long black coat flowing in the wind behind him rush onto the roof top.

Chester Stahl grabbed the microphone from the pilot of the transport and flipped on the external speakers.

"You're too late, Dragoon!" he shouted, his voice echoing over the park. "Your little attempt on my life failed!"

Stahl's eyes widened as the man pulled a large, triple-barreled weapon from behind his long coat and pointed up at him. He watched the man hesitate as the transport flew over the crowd, aiming his weapon right at Stahl. He took a deep breath as his transport drifted over the lake in the park. The moment Stahl realized why the man had hesitated, he knew it was too late.

Strange blue flames erupted from the under-barrel of the weapon the Dragoon was holding, spreading across the sky toward the transport. The tiny flaming thermite discs sliced into the sides of the hull and began melting through the metal. The ship evaporated around Stahl as more and more tiny discs cut deep into it, damaging the engines. To the pilot's credit, he managed to get the craft down into the lake before the melting metal consumed him.

Stahl managed to get out the rear door as four of his bodyguards melted away with the transport in the water. He and the two other survivors swam to shore, desperately looking for escape as citizens from the crowd encircled his location. Whether or not they were there to help or hang him was a debate Stahl would never have. One of the bodyguards opened fire with his pistol into the crowd.

Some people ran away from the shots, others ran toward him and his guards, overwhelming them. The last thing Councilman Chester Stahl saw were the furious eyes of the people who had come to hear him speak.

—

Watching the transport crash into the lake, the Dragoon turned and launched a barrage of small thermite discs at the rooftop exit he had come through. The stairs' metal housing began to melt into heavy molten drops as the Special Police squads ascended the stairs behind him.

Watching the riot unfold below, the man winced as shots were fired into the crowd by officers as they were getting overwhelmed. He knew it wouldn't end well, but he didn't have time to think about it too long. He could hear the sound of approaching helicopters and knew that he had to disappear soon.

The sound of the shot came after he heard the bullet whiz by his head. The sniper having misjudged the shot. The Dragoon didn't waste any more time.

With the exit behind him, full of soldiers as it continued melting away, the Dragoon ran as hard as he could toward the back of the building, up one side of a steep roof and down the other. The sound of bullets ricocheting around him pushed him to move faster.

When he got to the edge of the building, he used the power of his mechanized battle armor to leap the gap to the next building, rolling out of the momentum of the fall. As he got to his feet, he removed the latex pieces from his face that he had been using as a disguise, then turned and dusted off his suit before kicking through the roof exit access and disappearing down onto the street below.

The media would report on the riot for a full hour before getting orders to cease coverage. The government buildings in New York would go up in flames before the night was finished. In every major city in the world, the reaction was the same: the people watching the event grew furious at the exposure of the lies they had been told, and when the police began to fire upon the people, riots began to spread. Military and police forces around the globe were pressed to contain swarms of rioters.

History would remember it as the start of the Free Man Revolution.

CHAPTER 10

In a perfect world

IT WAS AN EARLY MORNING ON AERIS VII; THE SUN HAD barely crested the horizon when Marlena awoke. She and Alex were to meet with two men that morning who had arranged an appointment with them weeks before. In their home on what the locals had begun to call "Valhalla Island," the two greeted Doctor Franz Wagner and Earnest Evans, an engineer from the 3rd fleet who had arrived by way of a VS91-Transport Shuttle, which had set down on the landing pad between *Tizona* and *Skoll.*

Marlena greeted to two men, who had become acquaintances through their many discussions in her role as leader of the *Independents,* and introduced them to her son.

"As you know, we have twenty-one OMBI-solders held in our detention facility, gentlemen. I have examined the technology on my son's arm and have sent you both reports on what I have discovered. Alex has filled in the details on the removed inhibitor chips."

"I have read your report, Captain," the old, white-haired doctor said quietly, "and I am fascinated by the growing bond between the host and the device, as well as the bond he apparently has been forming with his ship."

"I want to know if it is dangerous to remove the 3rd inhibitor," Alex remarked eagerly.

"For now, I would leave it alone. The other inhibitors were to slow the development of the bond, but the third seems like it was intended to stay," Engineer Evans replied.

Evans had been an engineer since he was eighteen and had a knack for figuring out how things worked. The brown-haired man of forty-one had earned a reputation around Aeris VII for his ability to repair any device that was brought to him.

"Do you know how or why no one else can pilot *Skoll*?" Marlena asked, curious. She had been unable to find the answer herself, despite her extensive background with warships and technology.

"It's hard to say," Evans began, "but I have a theory that there may be some kind of virtual intelligence in the machine, which only recognizes one operator at a time. Actually, I believe that goes for the OMBI device as well."

"So you're saying that both the ship and my bracer have some kind of a consciousness?" Alex asked in awe.

"It's only a theory, Captain, but I believe so," Evans affirmed.

"When you develop your data on it, please forward it to me," Marlena said.

"Absolutely," Evans replied with a nod.

Doctor Wagner spoke up then, "It is curious how the 4th inhibitor works. Each time I proceed into the detention facility to speak with the children from Black Squadron, they collapse from nausea and accuse me of being a 'Gortha.'"

"I had a similar experience during the battle of the Eagle Nebula, Doctor. I could feel the inhibitor altering the data between my eyes and my brain, if that makes any sense," Alex added thoughtfully.

"I see. I think it would be good, at some point, to remove those inhibitors from the rest of your squadron; you may find yourselves some powerful allies in that group," Wagner commented, sharing a nod with Marlena.

"Thank you, Doctor, I will bring it before the ICC. I appreciate you both coming by. But if you'll excuse me, I have a preliminary council address to give," Marlena said, getting up and showing the men to the door.

—

Tizona had taken several hits during the battle, but the damage was light and Marlena had it repaired within two days. She left from her home that morning, after a preliminary conference with the Independent Council of Colonies. The Council had a great deal of agenda items, from current fleet distribution to casualties on the planet. Fortunately, with the attack happening at night, most of the officers and crew from the grounded Battle Frigates were in the city, so the majority of casualties happened on the two ships that were disabled in orbit.

Of the two frigates lost, two hundred and twenty-one crew members were labeled either KIA or MIA, representing about half from each vessel. Casualties on the other side of the conflict were substantially less; since *Skoll* disabled the ships efficiently, many lives were spared. The detainment facility was getting full on Aeris VII so naturally one of the top agenda items was the discussion of prisoner transfers.

Including the twenty-one OMBI-Soldiers of Black Squadron in custody, the prison facility housed nearly one thousand enemy troops. After the preliminary conference, Marlena nominated Alex as her proxy for the remainder of the issues and excused herself to make contact with her spy network on Earth.

When she arrived at the array, she was glad to see that it hadn't been attacked by any of the UEDF ships. She had gone to great lengths to conceal the location where she had built it and no one, other than she and Alex, knew where it was exactly. In her design of the array, Marlena used a slipstream generator to transfer the data more quickly. The stabilized wormhole could deliver messages nearly in real-time, since data seemed to move through the stream faster than matter. She also included a disrupter field that offered her both anonymity when transmitting and a minor cloaking ability for the array itself. She was proud of her work; nothing of its kind had been built before and it had only taken her fourteen months to complete.

As she landed *Tizona*, she shut down the engines and walked through her kitchen, pausing to pour coffee into a thermos. She mixed the dark liquid carefully with light cream and synthetic sugar, watching the mixture blend into a dark shade of brown before sealing it up. She was the kind of woman who expected excellence from herself, even with simple tasks.

Walking through her quarters, Marlena stopped, as she always did, to look at the pictures on her wall. On the wall was a picture of William poised thoughtfully over a set of blueprints with a pencil and T-square; in the photo he was looking up at her with a smile. She remembered the day that she took it, thinking about how proud she was of the man and his work. Tears rimmed her almond-colored eyes as she kissed her fingers and pressed them to the glass.

"I miss you, William," she said softly before moving on to the next photo.

The next one she stopped at was a picture of Alex and Connor sitting in a bathtub together as young boys. Connor had been eighteen months old in the photo and Alex had made him a soap-bubble beard, which he wore with a smile. Both boys had such sweet smiles that they made Marlena's heart ache.

Taking a deep breath, she grabbed her datapad and walked out of her room. She opened the airlock to the empty cargo hold and exited out the ramp onto the grassy hillside.

Walking over to the array, she felt a sense of anxiety, as she always did before these transmissions. She never knew what news to expect from Earth, but it wasn't normally good. Until she had both of her boys safely at home, and some kind of high-grade defensive armament around Aeris VII, she would never feel totally comfortable.

She went to her spot under a large tree, which had bright orange-colored leafs. She had put a rather comfortable wooden chair there to sit on while she communicated with Earth. Sitting down and taking a sip of her coffee, she activated the slipstream in the array. It took a couple of minutes to warm up and open the wormhole, but when it did, information from Earth began flooding her datapad.

She watched as headlines scrolled across the screen, naming Councilman Kaufmann and Councilman Stahl deceased as well as giving a name to their Murderer, "The Dragoon." The picture they showed was of a man dressed in a dark leather duster and wide-brimmed hat. Marlena thought he looked like a villain from a western movie as she scrolled through the story.

She was surprised to see that her own name was in the headlines, questioning the true motives behind her death and whether or not the Gortha were even real. Overwhelmed by the gravity of it all, she continued to read the story about the man who had exposed the current regime and the riots taking place in the major metropolis areas of Earth.

Terrorist lies, sedition and conspiracy theories:

"The death toll in the terrorist plot to murder Councilman Stahl has now been confirmed in the hundreds as special police scour the city in search of The Dragoon.

The number civilian casualties continues to rise as this terrorist's killing spree goes on. Notably, Councilmen Kaufmann and Stahl's deaths have both been attributed to the actions of a terrorist cell lead by The Dragoon.

From what we know so far, The Dragoon is a man in his mid 30's, who suffers from psychopathy and is highly trained in espionage and counter intelligence.

During the broadcast of Councilman Stahl's speech, The Dragoon ran a conspiracy, propaganda video regarding the Gortha attack in the Incident of 2115, which resulted in the death of Captain Marlena Mercer. The video errantly claimed that the UEDF cruisers turned on Captain Mercer; a claim which has been proven false by our fact checkers.

Also attributed to this terrorist cell is the rise of a new regime in the territory of Germany, which claims to be attempting to restore order in the region. To combat this threat, the UEDF has shut down the global power grid and access to food in the region, until this illegal government can be removed.

Riots in Eastern Europe and Asia have been suppressed by UEDF troops as terrorist cells spread the propaganda piece regarding the death of Captain Mercer."

Marlena was stunned by the news as she read. She had read enough news reports that she could see through the outright lies and found herself liking this Dragoon. She had hoped that the people of Earth would resist sooner or later, but she hadn't anticipated a global revolution springing up overnight, and in her name at that. Smiling, she began her transmission to Major Sanders.

—

Alex listened carefully as members of the ICC talked about fleet redistributions to protect Aeris VII. The commanders of the 3rd and 5th fleets were brilliant tacticians, and Alex found himself learning a lot while he listened to them discuss their strategy. Occasionally he would chime in with a remark, which would often be incorporated into the plans. Alex had a great eye for tactics and efficiency and was happy that he could offer positive input on the conference.

The commanders and civilian representatives were all extremely grateful for Alex's participation in the fight. They all had acknowledged, in turn, how he single-handedly turned the tide of the battle with his superlative skill and unique vessel. Alex accepted it all humbly, not wanting to make a bigger deal out of it than he had to. He was already well-known in the Independent Colonies as a hero from the Battle of the Eagle Nebula and he feared that too much recognition would put a lot of pressure on him to perform in the future. He was an excellent commander and a brilliant pilot, but Alex Pereira had no ambition to become an icon of a rebellion.

"Does anyone have anything to add before we close?" Commander Watson asked over the communicator.

"Actually, yeah, I do," Alex said, unsure of protocol.

"Go ahead, Captain Pereira." Watson sounded eager to hear what the boy had to say.

"On my way from Sapphire City to my ship, I encountered a man who tried to kill me, an operative of the EMC."

"You are sure it was an operative, Captain?" Commander Clarke asked carefully.

"Yes, sir, the man moved like a killer and was extremely well-trained. He identified himself as 'Operative One.'"

"If what you're saying is true, Captain, we have a serious problem here. The Operatives are espionage and assassination specialists, extremely well-trained at blending in. The fact that you survived is a miracle."

"Yes, sir," Alex agreed.

"We are all going to need to be very careful with an assassin loose on Aeris VII. We could all be targets." There was an edge of fear in Commander Clarke's voice.

"Would you be able to identify the man if you saw him, Captain?" Representative Gellar asked.

"I don't know; maybe. His features and clothing were very plain. Even the way he approached me was casual, not like what I would expect from someone so highly trained."

"Understood. Operatives are known for their ability to infiltrate. I doubt any of us will see him coming until he is attacking us," Commander Watson said sternly. "We must all take extra precautions for the time being to not let anyone we do not know near us, or give this assassin any clear shots. Thank you for letting us know, Captain."

"Sure. Anything I can do to help, Commander," Alex said respectfully.

He wasn't happy about the exchange. He had hoped that the ICC would have some kind of a solution or plan to deal with an operative. So, Alex resolved to be especially vigilant and hoped that none of the leaders of the Independent Colonies would be hurt. If he had another chance to stop Operative One, he would take it.

As the meeting adjourned, Alex felt himself getting restless at the thought of battling the operative again. Needing to take a break, he walked outside onto the patio with his datapad and wrote a message.

To: Lyria Shepherd

Subject: Dinner

Message: Dear Lyria, Sorry I haven't been around for the last couple of days. I had to help drag Frigates down from orbit and arrest their crews; exhausting work. I wanted to write you and let you know that I am okay and I am thinking about you. I know its short notice, but would you like to come over and have dinner with me tomorrow? I really want my Mom to meet you. Let me know.—Alex

-Message Sent-

Alex was two steps into the kitchen for a snack when his OMBI vibrated with the reply.

Message 1: Yes! Thank God you're alright. I've been worried. Pick me up at my place tomorrow at 7?—Lyria delivered 1000 2121-07-16 From: Lyria Shepherd

Alex wore a huge smile on his face as he replied.

To: Lyria Shepherd

Subject: Re: Dinner

Message: See you tomorrow at 7!—Alex

-Message Sent-

—

Major Sanders had been in his quarters all morning, dreading the transmission that he'd scheduled. When the light activated on his terminal, Sanders almost didn't answer it.

"Sanders here," he said reluctantly.

"Major, I've been getting reports from Earth that there are riots in the streets and the EMC has been exposed," The Shadow said to him in its distorted voice.

"I received the same reports. The Dragoon has really stirred things up. But the EMC is cracking down hard on the rioters. It could be an all-out massacre within a couple of weeks."

"I understand, Major. What is your report on our progress?"

112

Sanders hesitated too long.

"What happened?" The voice on the other end of the transmission sounded anxious.

"Connor Pereira is in the infirmary."

The silence lasted several seconds, the magnitude of the statement sinking in.

"Is he okay?" came the reply, concern evident even through the distortion.

"He has been unconscious since they found him, but he's stable. He was found in a training room within minutes of the incident, having been stunned and beaten by somebody. No one was supposed to use that room for two days, but oddly, every officer and staff member got an anonymous message on their datapad at exactly the same time informing them to proceed immediately to the room where he was. Even two AFMRs showed up."

"I see. Who was responsible?"

"No one has come forward. But, since there was no training scheduled, I suspect the Head Commander may have had something to do with it. The boy has enemies here, so it could have been several people."

"Listen to me. Find out who is responsible and report back to me."

The transmission ended abruptly, as it usually did. Sanders sat back at his console in deep thought. The incident had upset him too, but he couldn't just accuse the Head Commander of setting up a merciless beating of a ten-year-old boy.

—

Marlena Mercer sat under the orange-colored tree with tears in her eyes, all thoughts of the riots on Earth gone from her mind. The thought of her sweet son being hurt by somebody made her furious and she felt helpless being more than eight thousand light years from where she could do anything about it.

Her eyes looked back to her ship sitting nearby and, not for the first time, she thought about attempting to get to Earth. She knew, however, that she would be dead long before she got close no matter how accurate her slipstream jump was. She had tried once before right after the incident of 2115 and had barely escaped. From her contacts on Earth she knew that there was a standing "shoot on sight" order for her and her ship.

Frustrated and angry, Marlena screamed as loud as she could. Her voice echoed through the Grimnir Mountains for miles around, but no one was around to hear it.

CHAPTER 11

The wolf inside

THERE WAS NOTHING BUT WATER AS FAR AS THE EYE could see. Austin had been on the transport for the better part of an hour, heading toward a base where he was to receive special training, or so he had been told. Ever since he had been named the next candidate to be trained as an operative, he'd been transferred from base to base every day. In each place he was given a physical or psychological exam before he was moved to the next.

As the transport began its descent, Austin looked from the cabin out the front window to see a small landing pad in the middle of the ocean. He wondered what sort of exam they might give him on such a small platform. When the craft touched down, he was ordered to disembark by the pilot, who proceeded to lift off after Austin had gotten out.

He watched the transport fly away and wondered if someone had decided to play some kind of prank on him, since he was apparently alone in the middle of the ocean. He waited for several minutes until finally the platform shifted slightly, opening up to reveal a large tube-shaped lift. The airman upon the lift waved him over.

"Are you Corporal Hughes?"

Austin nodded.

"My orders are to take you down below. Get on the lift!"

When he stood on the lift, it began to descend through the platform into the ocean below. Once they were below the platform, the metal walls became glass and Austin watched as they plunged beneath the surface of the ocean, down into the dark depths. They continued downward for nearly five minutes until Austin saw lights below him. The underwater facility was made up of two large domed buildings, and several smaller domes around them. They were connected with short walkways that appeared to be made of glass.

When the lift reached the bottom, the doors opened and Austin was greeted by a man he had seen, but never met.

"It's a pleasure to meet you, Corporal Hughes," the man said slowly, sizing Austin up.

"Likewise, General Harruhama." Austin saluted the commander of the Earth Military Council.

"I understand that you have proven to be a loyal soldier to the UEDF, trying to stop your friend from betraying us."

"Yes, sir. Captain Pereira informed me of a malfunction in his OMBI and had me instruct an AFMR to remove a faulty inhibitor. I regret it now, sir. The removal of the inhibitor drove him insane," Austin said, giving the report to the best of his ability.

"It is a shame you could not stop him, he was a good soldier."

"Yes, sir, and a good friend."

The two began walking through the underwater halls of the facility, Harruhama leading Austin down a long corridor with the dark weight of the ocean on three sides.

"Do you know why you're here?" Harruhama continued.

"Operative training, sir," Austin replied confidently.

"Yes and no. Operatives are enhanced through a series of implants, making them faster, stronger, and more efficient combatants. You will receive these implants as well. But I have a different task in mind for you."

"What is that, sir?" Austin asked, perplexed.

"I need a solder that is capable of taking down a Battle Frigate or a Squad of Anubis Fighters. I need a soldier who can take down the *Skoll*, if necessary."

"That ship is unlike anything I have ever seen, sir."

"Then you will need a ship that is as unique," Harruhama said as he opened the door into one of the bigger domes.

In front of Austin was a large suit of armor that looked vaguely like *Skoll*, except where *Skoll* looked like a dragon-faced, black suit of samurai armor, this was a wolf-faced, white suit that looked like a 16th Century knight.

"This is *Hati*. I want you to try to operate it."

"*Hati* ... Okay, I will," Austin said reverently.

Austin walked around to the back of the kneeling Battle Armor Vessel and climbed inside. The cockpit was cramped and he could barely make himself fit into it. He forced his arms and legs in and reached out through his OMBI to the ship.

Nothing.

He tried again, concentrating on the intricacies of the vessel, reaching out to it. He could feel the power of the ship around him, and through his OMBI understood that this device would not work for him.

"Sir, I don't think I can pilot this ship," Austin said with no small amount of disappointment.

"Why is that, Corporal?"

"I can feel it, sir, through my OMBI. I am reaching out to it, it can hear me, but it's not obeying me."

"That is unfortunate," Harruhama said.

"Sorry, sir; I can try again if you like."

"No, that won't be necessary. We had suspected that it bonded to the previous pilot, but we wanted to be sure. We would have preferred for you to pilot *Hati*, but anticipating your failure, we have constructed another vessel."

Harruhama led Austin from the room into an adjacent dome where another Battle Armor Vessel waited. This one was far larger than *Hati* or *Skoll*, with massive arms and legs supporting a barrel chest. The Battle Suit Vessel was all red and looked like a suit of armor made for an ogre.

"Corporal, this is *Fenris*. A Battle Suit Vessel designed by the best engineers in the EMC, using specifications from the other two, to use your OMBI to interface with its weapons and navigation."

"Impressive," Austin said stoically as he walked up to the giant red ship. He had to climb up the massive legs to get aboard. As he settled in and slid his arms and legs into place, the thirty-foot-tall machine powered on.

Austin reached through his OMBI to *Fenris*, ordered it to move about the room slowly. The ship complied and took several weighted steps. It was slow and heavy, but Austin could feel the power surging through his bracer.

"I will let you two get acquainted. Report to the infirmary when you're ready to receive your enhancements; we have a lot of work to do, so don't wait too long," Harruhama said, smiling as he walked out the door.

—

He awoke to find himself lying near a small creek in the woods, the sound of rushing water drawing him from his nap. Connor didn't remember falling asleep here, but as he got up, he felt a sense of solitude. He knew the place; it was a ranch he had spent a couple of summers at with William learning how to shoot and ride horses. However, looking around, he could not see any structures or animals.

He walked along the creek bed, stumbling around rocks and fallen logs, looking for a way to higher ground so he could figure out where he was on the ranch. He didn't remember how he got that far out, but it seemed unlikely to him that he had walked. His confusion grew as he looked around for vehicle tracks but found none. Resolving to figure it out later, he walked on, until he came to an old road.

He walked up the road for nearly twenty minutes. His legs were sorer that he thought they should be as he climbed the hill up to where the houses were supposed to be located. When he got to the top, Connor was deeply saddened to find the beautiful log cabins and barns in ruins on the ground. There were no vehicles or people, just the ruins. By the look of them, they had been destroyed a long time ago.

Connor turned around to look out at the countryside and the mountains beyond. They were as pristine as he remembered, treed hills rolling up steep inclines to the high mountains that surrounded the valley. There wasn't a cloud in the sky and the summer sun felt warm on his skin. While looking around he spotted a strange figure on a nearby hill, known as "Lookout Point."

Connor remembered it well, because on a trip there with William, they had gone to the top to take pictures. But Connor, in an angry fit about something he couldn't remember, decided to take his shoes off and throw them as hard as he could. He chuckled at the memory of it now, of how childish his anger was back then.

The figure seemed like a tall man, and when Connor walked to the base of the hill, the man moved away from the edge where he had been standing. Connor began to climb, feeling his legs burning from the effort, each step causing labored breaths as he ascended the hill. When he got to the top, out of breath and hurting, Connor saw a familiar face of the ten-year-old version of William Mercer that Omega had used while training him.

"Omega?" Connor asked, uncertain.

"Good day, Initiator," Omega replied impassively.

"What are you doing at the ranch?"

"I am here with you." Omega replied as if it were obvious.

"Okay, but what happened to the houses?"

"They were destroyed."

"What are we supposed to do now?"

Omega pointed to a tall mountain off in the distance, the largest one they could see from the top of lookout point.

"That's great; we have to climb that?"

"The quest is about the journey, not the destination," Omega replied cryptically.

Connor tried to activate his OMBI to produce a vehicle, but with no success.

"We cannot travel that way in here, I'm afraid." A strange look of sympathy crossed Omega's face.

"Let's walk then," Connor said, taking a few steps toward the mountain. As he turned to tell Omega to follow him, he noticed that the hologram was gone.

"Well that was a lot of help," Connor quipped.

He descended back down to the creek the way he had come, and up the other side of the hill until he reached a long meadow and began to cross it, heading toward the mountain that Omega told him he had to climb. Along the way he noticed a picnic bench with a man sitting at it. As he approached, he recognized the face of his stepfather, William.

"William! I'm so glad you're here!" Connor said with excitement.

"Me too; glad you didn't forget about me," William said, a sad look in his eyes.

"I never could. You've been my best friend since I can remember!"

That made William smile, slightly diminishing the ever present wall of pain behind his eyes.

"Connor, I can't walk this path with you. It's going to be

hard and scary, but I want you to know that I believe in you. I have always believed in you."

William began to fade away like a wisp of smoke until Connor was alone again.

"I miss you, William," Connor said, tears rimming his chocolate-colored eyes.

When he got to the end of the meadow, Connor came to a wooded hill that he began to walk up. The trees were thick, and Connor kept thinking that he saw something out of the corner of his eye. Tired of being stalked, he stopped and spoke loudly.

"Whoever is there, just come out!"

"Calm down, Tons! I just wanted to see if you were paying attention!" Alex said with a boyish smile on his face as he walked out from behind a tree.

"Alex! Oh man, I missed you. I came after you when I heard that Black Squadron had been beaten, but you were gone!" Connor said, running to hug his brother.

Alex put his arms around his little brother tightly as he spoke. "I know you did, kid, I appreciate it!"

"Where did you go?"

"I can't tell you yet, but I want you to know something."

"What?"

"Don't believe everything you see," Alex warned as he began to fade away.

"I won't," Connor said, taking a deep breath before continuing up the mountain.

When he got to the top of the wooded hill, he could see the mountain rising ahead of him and he knew he was going to have to push himself to make it there by nightfall. He began to run through a rocky valley on his way to the base of the mountain. That was where he saw her, waiting for him.

"Hi, baby," Marlena greeted sweetly.

"Hi, Mom." Connor ran to hug her.

They embraced tightly, Marlena's hands tossing Connor's hair.

"Mom, I miss you every day!" Connor said, tears in his eyes for the second time that day.

"I miss you too, baby. I am so proud of you!" Marlena stared lovingly at her son.

"Do you have a message for me too?"

"Only that I love you, and when the time comes I'll be there for you." She said it so sincerely that Connor almost believed she wasn't dead.

As she began to dissipate Connor cried out.

"Mom, don't leave me!"

Tears were streaming down his cheeks as he ran to hold on to her. She looked back at him through glistening tears, fading away.

When she was gone Connor fell to the ground, sobbing. He sat there until the sun was low in the sky, unable to make himself stand to walk the rest of the way to the mountain.

He would have stayed there all night, but he heard a wolf howling in the distance. The sound echoed through the evening air, making Connor's skin crawl. Frightened, he got up and began to run up the side of the mountain, the sound of the wolf's cry getting closer.

His legs ached with increasing pain and his lungs felt like they would burst, but still he ran, trying to climb faster. He could hear the footfalls of the creature that was behind him. Soon, he could feel it's breath as it got close.

"Why do you run, Initiator?" the wolf asked into Connor's mind with a solid baritone voice.

"I'm afraid!" Connor cried out into the night air.

"You don't have to be afraid anymore, I am here."

"Who are you?" Connor asked, confused by why the telepathic wolf was not eating him.

"Hati, Initiator." The wolf dipped one leg in a regal canine bow.

"Well that makes a lot of sense! I guess I'm dreaming?" Connor stated, annoyed.

"Indeed. I have come to help you awaken," Hati said to him.

"Why can't I wake up?"

"You were injured badly. This is the first time in your life, but it will not be the last."

"That's comforting. What do you mean by that, anyway?" Connor asked, his voice oozing sarcasm.

"The time will come when they will try to kill us, Initiator."

"I don't want to die," Connor said quietly, putting his head down.

"Death is an inevitability of life," the wolf stated casually.

The two sat staring at each other for a minute until Connor turned and began walking back up the hill.

"Are you coming, Hati?" Connor asked, a smile appearing on his face.

Hati cocked his head to the side. "Affirmative; why do you smile?"

"Because it's all just a dream," Connor said cheerfully.

The wolf paused before continuing, "Indeed … it's all just a dream."

As the two ascended to the top of the mountain, Connor stood tall, reaching his arms out toward the moon that was rising into the sky. Hati howled and began to run toward the rising moon very quickly. Connor watched as the wolf grew in size and climbed a far-off mountain before leaping high into the sky. The wolf then swallowed the moon whole, leaving the world in darkness.

"Well that can't be good," Connor said with a little laugh.

⸺

"He spoke?" the doctor asked, coming into the room after being alerted by the attending 311AFMR.

"Affirmative, sir" the machine replied.

The doctor helped Connor sit up in his bed. "What did he say?"

"That can't be good," the machine repeated.

The robot and doctor began talking to Connor, who gave his best attempt at telling them where it hurt and how bad. He had sustained heavy injuries, but under the medical care of the Ombicademy staff and specialized machinery, he was recovering fast.

His left leg was broken, as well as his left arm, and his skull was cracked. All his injuries were being bonded with synthetic bone solution and he almost felt like he could walk out of there. The doctor informed him, however, that he would be unable to leave for a few days at least. He remembered who put him in the infirmary and how, and for the next few days Connor sat alone, plotting his revenge.

CHAPTER 12

Free Men

I

N THE HOURS SINCE THE RIOT BROKE OUT ON THE STREETS of New York, the Dragoon had been rallying groups of rioting citizens, using hit-and-run tactics against fortified special police positions. The local law enforcement and control personnel had attempted to contain the spreading riot by blocking off the broad streets of Manhattan. As the Dragoon and his forming army pushed them back, more and more squadrons arrived to contain the area.

It was public knowledge that the Dragoon had taken down Councilman Stahl's transport and assassinated Councilman Kaufmann by now, and the rioters had named him their leader as more and more citizens joined the cause. UEDF International Guard Squadrons began arriving within hours to help facilitate the capture of the man by closing off the city. The bridges and tunnels had been heavily fortified with heavy assault vehicles and a line had been formed at the edge of Harlem to the North. The choke points made it impossible for even larger groups of rioters to get in and out of the city, cutting off their ability to merge forces into a bigger army. It was clear that the EMC was trying to kill the Dragoon quickly to disrupt the man's influence on the people.

He had been holding captured UEDF and law enforcement

personnel in a downtown office building, keeping them comfortable and under heavy guard. To his surprise, once they had been removed from the battle, many of them had expressed sympathy for the cause and even offered to help. Naturally, nobody trusted them, but as the sentiment grew, the prisoners seemed content to just wait. When the Dragoon asked one of them why he wished to defect, he had said that Captain Marlena "Phoenix" Mercer was one of his idols growing up, and the fact that the EMC had killed her made him angry.

It was during that conversation that the Dragoon had come to realize he served as an inspiration for rioting, but that the woman would be a symbol for a revolution. He began using the battle cry, "Remember the Phoenix" before leading charges into heavily fortified areas. Always at the head of the charge, the Dragoon would run into battle like a man courting death. On several occasions, he charged alone into battles that no one should have walked away from, but somehow had come back out. The rioters, who began calling themselves "Free Men" spoke of him reverently, saying he was an angel, come down to judge the men who had enslaved the human race. The Dragoon made no effort to correct them.

On the second day after the death of Councilman Stahl, the UEDF radio chatter had begun to change. Previously they had been sending expeditions into the city to try to find the Dragoon. Having cooperative prisoners translating the code made their movements easy to predict and the man had successfully ambushed and captured three squads before they made it too far into the city. On that day, the translator had told him that the forces had been ordered to hold.

"What are they waiting for, Kyle?" The Dragoon had asked the short-haired boy, who had been a communications officer for the UEDF IG forces, before he had been taken prisoner. Kyle

Aaven seemed intelligent and willing to cooperate, so his interrogation seemed more like a collaboration.

"I can't say. Either they are going to make a massive push to kill us, or they are going to try to wait us out," Kyle said, hesitation evident in his voice.

Despite the news, the Dragoon smiled at the boy's usage of the word "us" when referring to the Free Men. Most of the people he had captured after meeting him felt like a part of the cause rather than the enemy.

"What are you thinking they will do?"

"Reports are coming in from across the globe; they have been trying to quell riots for three days. If I were Harruhama, I would do whatever it takes to remove the leadership of the Free Men as quickly as possible," Kyle offered thoughtfully.

"Agreed; I doubt they would risk an all-out assault. In the chaos, they might lose me. Plus, the troops, while better equipped, are severely outnumbered in an open fight."

"Then what, assassins?" Kyle asked.

"They have tried that before. I don't think so, too much ground to cover and how easy would it be for me to take off my mask and just blend in? Let me ask you something, kid, if you were a man who was dedicated to ruling humanity at any cost, and there was a threat to your rule, how would you remove him?" the Dragoon asked, already suspecting he knew the answer.

"Well, look what he did to the Phoenix in 2115? He was ready to sacrifice an entire colony to kill one woman in order to grab power."

The kid was smart.

"Orbital bombardment then, he means to kill everyone here to get to me."

"That seems likely. What are you going to do?" Kyle asked, concern written across his boyish features.

"Well, either I am going to have to give myself up or get out of town; staying here is only going to get people killed."

The kid stood up and saluted him.

"I understand. Good luck, sir."

The Dragoon thanked the boy and walked outside. This far from the barricades, few people were on the street. As the man walked east through the high walls of buildings, he looked up often to admire the old structures and the minds of the men who dreamed them up long before they were built. He'd always had an affinity for New York City, for humanity's achievement in its creation. He knew that the Free Men could easily hold this city against the forces of the UEDF so long as the orbital defense vessels didn't start firing downward, trying to eliminate him.

He knew that the best chance for the rebellion to take hold and eventually prevail would be for him to leave. He couldn't sneak out; it had to be publicly known. Anywhere he went from there would be at risk of bombardment from Battle Frigates in orbit, which meant he couldn't stay in one place long. Being an icon of a rebellion didn't seem so good anymore, but the man chuckled despite himself. He knew the EMC had to be removed from power if the people were to have any hope of being free and surviving the global resource shortage.

As he walked on the quiet streets, a plan began to form in his mind.

Later that same day, the Dragoon released all of his prisoners. Many had wanted to stay and fight on his side of the conflict, but he informed them that their insights and efforts would be far better served by returning to their command. With their hearts no longer with the EMC, it wouldn't be long before the sympathetic influence spread among the enemy forces. He knew he didn't have much time before the aerial bombardments began, so he organized a meeting in a large theater on Broadway with the men and women who had assumed rolls of leadership among the Free Men.

"Patriots," he began, addressing the room, "we have started down a road that will lead to the freedom of humanity."

The people in the room applauded as he continued.

"We have chosen this path to remove a corrupt power that has eroded our freedom, exhausted our resources, and has even taken our children all in the name of the 'greater good.'" His pitch rose as he spoke with growing passion to the assembled crowd.

"All around the world, men and women like you fight for the cause of liberty. Even now our enemy plans to launch an orbital strike on this city in order to kill me; that they may continue to rule and enslave you. They have underestimated your hearts and minds and they believe that if I am gone, you will not fight."

The crowd yelled, arguing the point.

"You have shown tremendous bravery, standing up to the EMC! We have thrown them out of this city, and it is time to push them from the borders as well. Without me in the city, the UEDF IG squads will have no reason to support the local troops, who are already beginning to lose their will to fight us."

The crowd got quiet. Everyone in the room held the Dragoon in high regard as a symbol of their cause, but each of them understood the truth of the matter. The city was theirs, as long as the Dragoon was not in it.

The man laid out his plans to get out of the city and put three trusted men in charge of leading the rebellion while he was gone. No one argued the point and the men who had taken on leadership roles seemed comfortable enough continuing the cause and keeping the EMC out of their city. They also agreed to support the surrounding areas in their efforts to liberate themselves. Plans in motion, the Dragoon focused on the long road ahead.

—

In the twilight hours of July 17th, the man called Dragoon loaded his three-barrel shotgun, then got onto his motorcycle on Essex Street, patiently waiting. He took several deep breathes, reminding himself that he had gotten through worse in his life than what he was about the face. He let his mind drift away from the task at hand while he waited for the signal to begin his run.

In his mind he thought back to the life he had before becoming a vigilante freedom fighter. It hadn't been more than a few months, but in his heart, it felt like a lifetime. When he thought about his past, his mind always went to the same moment, the day he had met the woman he would marry.

It seemed like such a minor detail at the time; he was out of synthetic creamer for his coffee. He almost used milk and sugar, but that particular Saturday morning, he got the strong urge for hazelnut. He traveled to the local market, which, as fate would have it, had been out of the hazelnut flavor that he wanted. So he got back into his red truck and continued to the other side of town, now on a quest for the right creamer. It became a game to him, and he even paused to wonder why fate would deprive him of such a simple pleasure.

He arrived at the market and strode boldly toward the refrigerated section at the back of this store that he had never been to. As luck would have it, there was one bottle left of the particular creamer he craved. As he removed it from the cooler he heard a melodic voice from behind him.

"Oh, last one, eh?" she said, the first words she spoke to him.

He turned to see the most stunning women he had ever laid eyes on. Her long dark hair fell casually across her shoulders as she held a baby in her arms while her young son pushed the grocery cart. As he looked into her almond-colored eyes, the two smiled at each other.

"Yeah, I guess it is," he managed to sputter out.

Their eyes remained locked on each other, neither talking for several moments. It was the woman's son who broke the silence.

"Mom, can I get chocolate milk?"

"Yes, Alex, but only a small one," she had said.

"Here" he said, handing her the creamer while her son climbed into the refrigerator, ascending the racks to get his chocolate milk.

"No, you got it first. But thank you," she replied, still looking into his dark-blue eyes.

"I insist." He was unable to look away. Her dark hair framed the most beautiful face he had ever seen.

"Tell you what; I'll split it with you." A smiling formed on her lips.

"Are you inviting me over for coffee miss?" he asked, sharing her smile.

"I guess I am," she replied, "I'm Marlena."

"William Mercer. It's really nice to meet you, Marlena."

The gravity between them was apparent from the first word and had only grown with time. He was in love with her by the time they left the market. A year later, they would be married and making plans to build a house together.

He had never been as happy as he was back then. His life before her seemed like empty space, despite his many achievements. He grew to love her children and raised them with the dedication and patience of a caring father. He remembered the times they would travel together, seeing new things for the first time as a family, excited every day to see what life would offer them next.

In those moments he made up his mind on where he would go from New York: to rescue his adopted son.

An explosion in the distance tore the man from his thoughts. Tears were streaming down his face as he started the ignition of his motorcycle.

"I miss you, baby," William said to the evening air, kissing the gold wedding band he still wore.

He revved his engine a few times to get the motor hot then dropped it into first gear, spinning the tires and accelerating around the corner onto Delancey Street, heading east. The Williamsburg Bridge loomed head, a fortified stronghold of the UEDF troops.

As he sped up, he weaved around the k-rail barricades toward the makeshift walls the International Guard had set up on the bridge. The rockets that the rebels had liberated from a supply depot in the city soared in over his head, striking the wall, scattering the defenders onto the bridge, disoriented. Using his left hand, William removed his triple-barreled shotgun and launched both barrels' worth of explosive pellets in a barrage of concussive destruction at one of the weak points created by the rocket fire.

The wall split apart as the man and his motorcycle tore through to the other side. It took the surprised troops on the other side a few moments to realize what happened and to recognize the man who had pierced their defenses. They began to call in his location and description more quickly than he hoped, some even raising their weapons and shooting in his direction as he sped away.

He'd heard the EMC forces had turned the local airports into makeshift transport hubs for troops coming into the city to quell the rebellion. He knew he had about an eight-mile span to cross, before he would reach what had been JFK International Airport. The riots on this side of the bridges had not been as effective as they had been in Manhattan and troops moved to block and attack him as he traversed the otherwise desolate urban landscape.

He was traveling recklessly fast, making hairpin turns to avoid roadblocks, occasionally feeling the sting of small arms fire upon the battle suit he wore beneath his duster. As he neared the halfway point of his run, the roadblocks didn't seem as prepared for approaching vehicles, and as he rounded the corner onto Atlantic Avenue he sped up to run through the unprepared checkpoint. He noticed that the area around him was getting brighter, like a huge spotlight was focusing on his location. He knew what it meant, and pulled his throttle back as hard as he could, turning down a side street just before the checkpoint.

The road block and its guards erupted in a massive explosion, the shockwave nearly knocking William from his bike even though he was nearly a block away. They had targeted his egress from orbit, and the Battle Frigates had begun a bombardment, trying to end his life as desperately as they could. The bright lights came down like rain as night descended upon the city. Buildings burst outwards from the cannon fire as the man swerved and dodged the best he could. He knew the gunners aboard the Battle Frigates, high above his location, were good, and it wouldn't be long before they anticipated his evasion well enough to get him.

Frustrated that his enemy was willing to sacrifice their own troops and innocent lives, the man wondered if they would even sacrifice the transportation hub to get to him. As he neared JFK International, he noticed a large checkpoint at the entrance and slowed down. He waited until the light began to form around him again before speeding up directly at the gate, counting the seconds before the orbital weapon would impact.

It was a guess. They had been landing between four and six seconds of the light. Using five as his number, he went full speed at the roadblock.

Four. The soldiers ahead, noticing the light, began frantically running to the sides, abandoning their positions. William focused intently on maintaining his speed.

Three. He felt the air around him heating up, knowing that impact was eminent now, tracking his motion from orbit, anticipating his path.

Two. Small stones and rubble on the expressway began to lift off the ground as the energy of the cannon forced gravity to shift; he even felt himself tugged slightly upwards.

One. Fully committed to his plan and counting on his battle suit to absorb the impact, the man leaped backwards off his motorcycle, trying to use his enhanced legs to slow his momentum or turn it to the side. He felt his ankle crush under the momentum of his body and the ground rush up to meet him.

Zero. The checkpoint exploded in flames, consuming the soldiers that had been there and the motorcycle the man had been riding for the past several months. The explosion flung him back, against the momentum of his roll, the concussion whipping his head violently into the ground. The helmet he wore absorbed the impact, but knocked him unconscious as he rolled to a stop under a small bridge.

—

From orbit, the ATG Gunner of the UEDF Battle Frigate Paladin watched his monitor carefully. He had been tracking the movement of the terrorist since his run began over the Williamsburg Bridge. He was glad that he hadn't had to level the city with the other frigates to kill the man; although, he had been briefed on that contingency. He had a nephew who lived in Soho, and the idea of destroying an entire city to kill one man left a bad taste in his mouth.

As it was, he had probably killed more people trying to take down the one man than he cared to admit to himself. On his motion anticipation monitor, he watched as the man's signal went dead in the checkpoint that had erupted around him.

"Well, Sergeant?" his commander asked.

"Target eliminated, sir. No movement."

CHAPTER 13

Better left unsaid

EIGHT THOUSAND LIGHT YEARS AWAY FROM WHERE THE battles raged on the streets of Earth, Marlena Mercer and her son Alex Pereira were watching through a one-way glass window at the interrogation of Captain Balvoon of the UEDF Battle Frigate *Cortez*. The man had been uncooperative, despite the decent treatment he had been receiving at the hands of his captors.

The interrogator had been gently prodding until now, asking forceful questions about the intent and targets of the attack on Aeris VII. The captain of the *Cortez* did not give one piece of valuable information. Frustrated, the interrogator left the room.

"Mom, let me go in there, I can break this guy," Alex said, not taking his eyes off of Captain Balvoon.

"Is that right? Does your OMBI have some mind-reading function that I don't know about?" Marlena asked, forcing a smile.

Alex had been in a bad mood ever since she told him about Connor's condition at the Ombicademy. She had to physically stop him from boarding *Skoll* and leaving for Earth. They knew they needed a plan if they were ever going to get anywhere near the Ombicademy and the argument about it was getting old fast.

"No, but it does have this." Alex manifested a black dagger in his hand.

"You know that he is a captain and has been trained to resist torture. Do you really think you have the stomach to do what it takes, Alex?" she asked seriously. She was afraid that his answer would be yes.

"I guess not. I'm tired of waiting while Connor is hurt in a bed somewhere and the people of Earth are rebelling. Here we are, standing around in an air-conditioned room while others are out there fighting!"

The passion was evident in his voice, and at that moment Marlena was extremely proud of her son.

"You're right. I'm going to go talk to Balvoon." Rising, she exited the room.

She passed the interrogator in the hallway and waved him off when he tried to follow her into the holding cell.

"Well, you're a pretty thing; did they send you in there to tempt information out of me?" Balvoon said with a lascivious smile on his face.

Her fist connected with his face before he knew it was coming. The man's head whipped back, blood streaming from his nose. He looked back at her, stunned that she had struck him.

"Now that we understand each other, Captain Balvoon," she said quietly.

"How dare you strike a prisoner? I am an officer in the-"

He was silenced by her fist as it plunged into his nose again.

"I can do this all day," she said, smiling.

"What do you want?"

"I want you to tell me why you attacked us."

"Go to hell. You can hit me all you want; I am not a traitor like you."

Marlena crossed her arms. "Let's talk about that. Do you know who I am?"

"Should I?" He looked closer at her face, genuine confusion apparent in his voice.

"Yes. I am Captain Marlena Mercer. Call sign: Phoenix."

"I don't believe you. Captain Mercer died in the incident of 2115!"

"Fighting the Gortha, I know. How many Gortha have you battled, Captain? How many enemy ships have you defeated protecting the colonies?"

"What does that have to do with it?"

"You came out here to subjugate colonists and destroy a rebel faction, you must have known that much. But how many Gortha have you seen, or even heard of firsthand?"

The man sat and thought for a long time, before he finally understood what this woman was saying.

"So you're saying that there are no Gortha, that they were invented by the EMC?" Balvoon asked, the edge of skepticism in his voice.

"I'm telling you to trust your own eyes, Captain. Do we look like a hostile enemy force to you? Or do we look like a peaceful colony that doesn't want to be oppressed by an overreaching militaristic government?"

The logic was hard for Captain Balvoon to ignore. He had always been the kind of man who accepted his orders without asking questions. But now that the information was apparent, he had trouble closing his mind to it.

"Listen, my job was to strike this colony while it was unprepared to disable the military targets and identify the leaders of the rebel faction. If we were successful, we were intended to occupy this planet until supply ships could come and acquire resources. If we failed, the plan was to send a much larger force to attack Aeris to eliminate the resistance to UEDF rule."

Marlena nodded along the entire time, listening to this man tell her the details of his mission.

"So you're saying that a larger force is on its way?"

"Not yet. We were supposed to broadcast a message before we retreated, however your … fighter, or whatever it was, had begun disabling us so quickly that we didn't have the chance. The ships currently in slip stream will be carrying that message."

"Thank you, Captain. I will be sure to see to it that you continue to receive fair treatment while you're our guest here."

She got up to leave, pausing at the door when the man began to speak.

"Are you really, Phoenix?" he asked, sounding genuinely curious.

"Yes," she replied as she shut the door behind her, leaving a stunned Captain Balvoon alone to question everything he believed in.

⌒

Lyria Shepherd was closing up the Cerulean Sky Café, getting ready to head home to change for her date with Alex. Butterflies were in her stomach as she thought about the boy's striking green eyes and the way he looked at her. She was so entranced that she almost didn't see the man walking up behind her.

"Excuse me," he muttered.

Startled, she jumped slightly.

"You scared me!" she yelled as she put her back against the door of her café.

"My apologies, miss. I did not mean to startle you."

"It's okay. Was there something you needed? We're closed for the day."

"Oh no, it's just that I am new in Sapphire City. I arrived

from the Carina Nebula Colony a few days before that attack." The man's plain features formed a smile.

"It's normally not like that. Just bad timing, Mr…"

"Gasper, Earnest Gasper. It's nice to meet you."

"Likewise, Mr. Gasper; I'm Lyria, owner of the Cerulean Sky Café."

"Yes, I have heard that you have a first-rate establishment. The reason I stopped you is because I came to Aeris VII because of the wide array of metals discovered here. I am a jeweler by trade, and wanted to open up a shop in downtown Sapphire City."

"It's a busy location. If your product is good, you should do very well here," she said, smiling at her fellow entrepreneur.

"Well yes, I believe so. I wanted to ask if you would be willing to wear a pendant I fashioned, that I may develop my clientele through word of mouth, if it pleases you."

While the man spoke he produced a blue sapphire pendent from his coat. The silver chain glittered in the waning daylight as the man twirled the gemstone.

"It's beautiful; I would be honored to wear it!" Lyria said excitedly.

"That makes me happy! Thank you!" he said as he clasped the necklace around her neck. "It suits you."

"Thank you, Mr. Gasper. I look forward to seeing the rest of your work when you open your shop! But if you'll excuse me, I am running late!" With a quick wave, she turned and walked down the street toward her apartment.

"It's really my pleasure," the man called out, watching her go. It had been an expensive gift, but he knew it would be paying dividends before the night was through.

Alex arrived at 7pm sharp to pick Lyria up for their dinner date. He was wearing a blue collared shirt and black slacks. He hadn't dressed up for anything in years, more accustomed to wearing a flight suit or uniform than civilian clothes.

Adjusting his collar, he rang the bell and, after a moment, Lyria came down the stairs to open the door. Alex was stunned by how beautiful she looked. Her hair was in curls, bouncing as she walked. The blue pendant complemented her eyes and the yellow dress she wore made her look like a princess to Alex. He was glad that he wore something nice at that moment.

"You look beautiful," Alex stammered as she opened the door.

"Thank you. You look very handsome as well!" she said, beaming.

The two walked hand in hand toward the docks, saying nothing and blushing each time they looked at each other. Alex could feel her soft fingers in his hand as he led her to his boat. They both had butterflies in their stomachs as he helped her aboard.

She watched him as he expertly piloted the boat out into the open water. Standing next to him, arms linked together at the elbow, it all felt like a dream, the way the boat glided across the water that evening as the two moons of Aeris VII rose above the horizon. She moved closer to him, resting her head on his shoulder. Alex could smell the scent of strawberries in her hair, making him feel weak in the knees.

When they arrived at the island's small dock, Alex took Lyria by the hand and steadied her as she stepped off the boat. They walked slowly to the house, enjoying each other's company.

They proceeded through the side door, past the study, and into the kitchen where Marlena was preparing dinner. By the smell of it, Alex could tell that dinner would not disappoint.

"Mom, this is Lyria Shepherd," he said, unsure of exactly how to introduce her.

"Hi! I'm Marlena, Alex's mom. It's nice to meet you, Lyria; I've heard a lot of nice things about you." She was sincere, but the edge of frustration still lingered in her voice from the news they had received that day.

Alex had pleaded with her to put aside leading the Independent Colonies for one night so he could introduce his girlfriend to her. Marlena agreed tentatively, wanting her son to be happy. She had told him that it wasn't a good time for romance with the way things had been heating up with the UEDF, but also conceded that there might never be a good time, so he should enjoy it while he could.

"It's a pleasure to make your acquaintance, Marlena. Alex has told me a lot about you too. Thank you for saving my life," Lyria replied, matching Marlena's sincerity.

"What do you mean?"

"I was only eleven when my aunt and I signed up to be a part of the Andromeda expedition to colonize this planet. After we landed and came out of stasis, I heard that you had saved us all. I had always hoped I would meet you so I could thank you. You are an icon to women all over the planet; it really is an honor to have dinner with two heroes." She looked from Marlena to Alex.

"She sounds like a keeper, Alex," Marlena said with a grin. "It was my pleasure, Lyria."

As they ate the dinner Marlena had made, the three talked about life on Earth before the colonization of Aeris. Some of the stories were about her deceased parents or William, which they told sadly. Alex even talked about Connor a little bit, and expressed his frustration and desire to retrieve his little brother.

As the night went on the conversation evolved to the plan they had been cooking up since before Alex left to pick the girl up. They had agreed to not discuss it at dinner, but once they started talking about Connor and Earth, it was unavoidable.

"If we use Skoll's slipstream, we should be able to get ahead of the convoy!" Alex said excitedly. "If we're waiting for them when they arrive, we could stop them from requesting reinforcements."

"At least until we get better orbital defenses around Aeris," Marlena agreed.

"It sounds risky. Are you sure that just two ships can defeat half a battle group?" Lyria asked as she ate. She wasn't versed in military strategy, but she knew that battle groups tended to be powerful.

Alex and Marlena looked at each other and grinned. It was Marlena who answered.

"It shouldn't be a problem."

"How long does it take to get to Earth with Skoll?" Lyria asked, looking at Alex.

"A couple weeks there, a couple weeks back. I shouldn't be gone for that long," he replied taking her hand.

"Easy for you to say. It won't feel like any time has passed for you."

Alex shrugged.

"I am just concerned that we will be very close to Earth when we come out of the slipstream. If we are detected, Harruhama will hit us with everything he has," Marlena interjected.

"If we can stop them though, the full invasion of Aeris might never happen. It's worth the risk," Alex offered. "Also if we're that close to Earth, maybe we can get Tons…"

"No!" Marlena said suddenly. "I want to get him just as much as you do Alex, but we cannot risk it. I tried going to Earth once before, in 2115. I didn't even get close before I was nearly shot down. The orbital defenses are too strong."

"I know. I'm just worried about him," Alex said, backing down.

Shortly after, with the night getting late and with a lot to do before the mission, Marlena excused herself and went into her room upstairs to develop a strategy for defending Aeris in her absence.

Alex and Lyria walked around the small island, stopping occasionally to throw rocks into the water.

"What do you think you'll do when the war is over?" Lyria asked Alex, breaking the silence.

"I don't know," he replied, as if he had never thought about it. "My entire life since 2115 has been about avenging my mom. I have never thought about what I would do after that. What about you?"

"Up until a couple weeks ago, there was no war that we were aware of. I just figured I would run my café, until I met you. Now, I don't know," she replied thoughtfully.

"When I was a kid, I always wanted to play baseball. I would love to do that. Although..." He trailed off.

"What?" She asked.

"It's just this," Alex said, holding up his right arm, manifesting a bat into his hand. "I don't think there is a league that would take an enhanced player."

To prove his point, he grabbed a small stone off the ground and shut his eyes as he tossed it into the air. He swung the bat, perfectly connecting with the stone sending it soaring out of sight. They didn't even hear it hit the water.

"Oh. I see," Lyria said, sounding sad as Alex let the bat dissipate.

"Maybe we can travel? See the other colonies! Aeris is way different from Hades and Earth, I bet some of the other colonies are amazing too," Alex said, excitement building in his voice.

"I would love that! I have always wondered what the others were like! Let's do it!" Lyria exclaimed, matching his excitement.

The two smiled at each other. They were all smiles as the evening moved to playful topics. The moons were high in the sky when Alex took Lyria back to her apartment.

"I had a great time tonight. Your mom is really sweet and so pretty!" Lyria said, smiling at Alex.

"Thank you. I think so too. I had fun; we really should do this again when I get back."

The reminder that he was going to be away for a while put a sour note on the evening. Even so, Lyria was not about to let it completely spoil her night. She leaned into Alex and snuggled up close. Alex held her in his arms for a long while, breathing in the scent of her hair, letting it take his mind off the impending mission and his time away.

That night the air was cool and the light from the two moons of Aeris VII illuminated the city in a soft, magical glow. Alex smiled at Lyria for a moment before kissing her in the moonlight.

⁓

Earnest Gasper was sitting in his apartment listening to the young lovers through the transmitter he had placed in the necklace that he had given to the girl. He rolled his eyes over the romantic rhetoric as he read through the transcript of the plan to ambush the convey returning to Earth. He opened his datapad to type.

To: General Harruhama

Subject: Aeris Invasion Failure

message: General, the invasion of Aeris is a failure. Launch the fleet with all possible haste, defenses are weak. Captain Mercer and her son are planning an ambush on the returning vessels. Attached are the coordinates, do not underestimate them.— Operative One

-Message encrypted / message sent-

The man leaned back in his chair, looking out the window over the waters of Lake Amsvartnir, a sinister plan forming in his mind.

CHAPTER 14

Vengeance

C ONNOR HAD BEEN IN THE INFIRMARY FOR SIX DAYS
when the doctor allowed his release. He'd been lying
in bed, bored as can be while the synthetic bonding
agent strengthened his bones enough for him to proceed with
normal training. During that time he managed to pull up various
bits of data using his OMBI regarding the global unrest that was
taking place.

Connor even accessed video from some of the Dragoon's
raids. Using the OMBI to access closed networks and security
was getting easier for him each time he attempted to dig around
for information. He watched the man, alone, raiding a supply
depot in the Midwest, shooting his strange shotgun at targets
off camera. At first, Connor didn't know what to make of the
man; the media had reported him a murderer and a terrorist,
but Connor thought he was brave for standing up alone against
the entire UEDF. As he read the man's exploits against the leadership of the EMC, he came to admire the Dragoon.

Naturally, a student of the UEDF Ombicademy shouldn't
be a fan of a revolutionary, so Connor decided to keep his opinion about it to himself. With days of waiting, Connor also decided that he needed to pay back the people who had set him
up. Using his OMBI, he accessed various mail accounts to find

out that Johnny had come up with the idea, which the Head Commander supported. Apparently Vector was mostly innocent in the planning, despite his aggressiveness and actions that nearly killed Connor.

He had decided from the moment he woke up that everyone involved would need to experience at least as much pain as he did. He figured he would start with the lieutenants of Red Army, since it would put the others on high alert, making their downfall that much sweeter. He spent a lot of time accessing various video feeds from around the Ombicademy, learning the patterns and routines of his soon-to-be victims.

The morning he was released, he was watching a video feed of George "Hammer" Brink lumbering alone down the hallway toward the gym. Connor didn't waste any time, walking immediately to the gym and then back toward the Red Army barracks.

When Hammer saw him in the hallway heading right at him, he actually stopped for a moment and then turned to run. Connor caught up to him quickly and, with a diving tackle, knocked Hammer to the ground.

"What do you want?" Hammer stammered.

Connor grinned as he slammed his fist into Hammer's nose. He knew the kid was most likely just along for the ride, but he hit him a few more times anyway, until Hammer was unconscious. He grabbed Hammer's OMBI and wrote a message:

To: Michael Jenner; Russell Faulkner

Subject: New Training Room!

Message: I just found a new training room by the Gym. It opened for me, you guys should come check it out; it's very cool!—Hammer

-Message Sent-

Connor wasn't sure if that sounded like Hammer at all, but he got up and continued to walk toward the Red Army Barracks. Fortunately his ruse paid off when he got nearly to the barrack entrance; Mikey "Rat" Jenner and Russell "Snake" Faulkner were just leaving. They didn't see Connor at first, so he followed them as they walked down the metal corridors toward the gym.

When they got to where Hammer was lying unconscious, they began to look around. They saw Connor too late to escape his trap. He was running full speed down the hallway toward them. As they stood up, Connor leapt into the air between them, kicking out with one leg as he spun, connecting to Rat's face and then the back of Snake's head. The boys both fell in opposite directions. When Connor's feet touched the ground, he reversed his direction, coming back on Rat, pummeling him with his fists so quickly that the Red Army Lieutenant could not hope to block him.

When Rat was unconscious, Connor turned to find Russell curled up in a ball on the floor, pretending to be unconscious too. Connor didn't hesitate kicking the kid several times until all three boys were knocked out and bleeding on the ground.

"Okay okay, apology accepted," Connor said sarcastically, grinning as he walked away.

On his way back to his barracks, Connor began looking up video feeds, trying to locate Johnny. As it turned out, Johnny was sitting on his bunk in the Red Army barracks playing some kind of game on his OMBI. Connor thought to use the same message trick he used to lure out Rat and Snake; however, he thought Johnny's punishment should be more public.

He walked back to the Red Army barracks door, and opened it using his OMBI. Normally kids from other armies weren't allowed in each other's barracks, but Connor thought that was a stupid rule, considering the doors were so easy to open.

He marveled how differently Red Army maintained their

living quarters, not bothering to clean up after themselves. Blue Army's barracks were not always immaculate by any means, but at least they didn't have garbage piled up in the corners. Members of the older classes of Red Army were sitting in the common room talking, seeming oblivious to Connor's entry. He walked slowly, so he wouldn't draw attention as he approached the 2126 barracks.

Many soldiers were sitting on their beds, wasting their day. Connor wasn't surprised that Red Army wasn't very good, these kids were lazy. Even while Connor was out getting payback, Blue Army was in the gym on their side of the Ombicademy, growing stronger. For a moment Connor thought he should teach every kid in these barracks a lesson on why training was important.

"Hey, you're not supposed to be here," a girl's voice said from a bunk near the door.

Connor turned his head to regard the brown-haired girl. She was plump, no doubt from spending the last several months living like they were in Red Army. Other kids began looking up, none moving to stop Connor's progress as he stalked toward Johnny. One of the kids made the effort to call out a warning to his commander before Connor had crossed the room.

Looking up, Johnny was immediately on his feet, searching for an escape route.

"Red Army, attack him!" Johnny cried out to his soldiers.

No one got up. They didn't take orders outside of the arena, apparently.

"Someone, help!" Johnny yelled, hoping that someone would rescue him.

Connor walked slowly, a smile forming on his face as he got closer to Johnny. He found himself enjoying the kid's terror. When he was within a few steps, Johnny's tone changed.

"I'm sorry, Connor! I didn't think Vector would hurt you that bad. We were just going to try to teach you a lesson! Don't hurt me!" Johnny's voice told everyone in the room that he was on the edge of panic.

Connor stopped and laughed.

"What was the lesson that you were going to teach me?" Connor asked, feigning interest.

"Just that no one should be so good at anything!" Johnny cried, his voice pleading for mercy.

"Johnny, in all my life, I have never heard anything so stupid."

"What are you going to do?" Johnny asked.

"Teach you a lesson about teaching lessons."

By that evening, Johnny and his lieutenants were in the infirmary and Red Army would have to forfeit its next match against Green Army. Connor had waited for the disciplinary message to come his way, but by the next morning he had given up on the idea that he would get the opportunity to go toe to toe with the Head Commander over the incident.

He was talking to Cat and Ladder the next morning about what happened when his OMBI flashed with a message.

Message 1: Report to Observation Lounge "Conscript Pereira is to report to the Observation Lounge immediately" delivered 0730 2121-07-20 From: Major Sanders

"Great," Connor said, sounding miserable.

"What is it, Connor?" Concern was etched in Cat's voice from where she sat at the foot of Connor's bunk.

Connor smirked. "Just got called to the principal's office."

Ladder and Cat chuckled a bit at that.

"Do you think you're going to get in trouble for beating up Red Army?" Ladder asked, sitting on the floor.

"I don't think so. They didn't get in trouble for beating me up. Besides, it was Major Wolf-Face Sanders that called me up, not the Head Commander. Last time I got a message like this, I got only bad news." Connor grimaced at the memory.

"I'm sure it will be fine. Want me to walk with you to the lift?" Cat asked, smiling.

"Yeah sure, Cat." Connor grinned back.

The two held hands in the hallway while they walked. Connor had found out that Cat had tried to visit with him in the infirmary but was denied access. She even had faked an injury to try to get in, but the 311-AFMR wouldn't approve her injury as valid. When she got word that Connor was awake, she waited patiently for him to return. He had missed a battle when he was out, but he hadn't asked about it. Connor didn't seem to care about that sort of thing anymore.

They took the long way, opting to walk slowly before finally arriving at the lift. The airman, having been humiliated by Connor before, stepped aside without asking him his business. Connor glared at the man anyway, for good measure.

Before going up, Cat kissed him on the cheek softly and said, "Good luck, Commander."

She was blushing and running back to the Blue Army barracks before Connor had a chance to reply. He had really come to like the girl and found himself enjoying the familiar confusion of how he was supposed to act around her. He shrugged as the lift proceeded upward, focusing on what awaited him at the top. He'd played it off to his friends that he wouldn't get in trouble, but the truth was, Connor was afraid he was going to face a severe punishment.

As the lift arrived at the top, two armed guards were waiting for him. They flanked him as he stepped forward, looking at a smirking administrator.

"Keep smiling, maybe it'll be your lucky day and they'll shoot me," Connor said to her snidely.

The woman's smile grew as the guards escorted him into the observation lounge.

The scene was not what Connor had expected. Instead of

an angry Head Commander, an old Japanese man in a general's uniform was sitting behind the desk. Major Sanders was standing to one side quietly, and nodded slightly at Connor as he walked through the door. Connor found himself nodding back, despite not liking the man.

Ten other guards were in the room, all armed and staring at Connor as he walked in. Connor stopped in front of the desk, looking into the eyes of an old man who was peering back at him, sizing Connor up, carefully weighing what he would say. It occurred to Connor that the man might be waiting for him to salute, but he wasn't going to give him the pleasure.

"Well, you got me here. What can I do for you?" Connor asked, breaking the silence. One of the guards coughed loudly, sounding surprised.

"I heard that you had a lot of spirit. Of course, you would have to, to break out of the Ombicademy, steal a ship, overwhelm four armies in a battle, and threaten your Head Commander," the man said, eying Connor carefully.

"I guess I don't need to introduce myself then. But who are you?" Connor asked.

"I am General Harruhama," the man stated matter-of-factly.

"I have heard that you have a lot of spirit, General. Of course, you would need to, to take over a world government, command all the fleets, and rule a galactic government," Connor quipped, trying to match the general's tone.

Connor thought he heard Major Sanders gasp. The room was quiet as the man stared at the boy. After a moment, a smile spread across General Harruhama's lips. Then he did what no one in the room had ever seen before: the general laughed.

"I like this kid," he said mirthfully, looking back at Sanders, who just shrugged in reply.

The general continued as his laughter died down, "They

tell me you're way ahead of your classmates. I would like to see what you got."

Connor smiled, an idea forming instantly in his mind. "Can I make a suggestion?"

"By all means."

"There is a former student in the Academy named Vector. He was one of the top soldiers in Black Army 2121. Let me spar him one on one, in an arena or training room, and I'll show you how good I am."

"Vector has had two of his inhibitors removed already. His arsenal is lethal; it would be irresponsible to allow such a one-sided match," Sanders said, speaking up.

"If you want it to be fairer, you can bring in all of Black Army, but I still think it might be one-sided," Connor said confidently.

Another smile formed on the general's lips as he replied, "I cannot tell if you are arrogant or confident, Pereira."

Connor fists clenched at his sides. "Set up the fight and you'll see."

"Very well, Major, please summon Private Wick to training room eleven."

Sanders was typing the message on his datapad before the general finished speaking. After it was sent, the general, the major, twelve guards, and Connor proceeded to the lower levels toward the training dojo that Connor had spent so much time in.

When he got inside, Connor felt a little like he had come home. The dojo actually reminded him a lot of the one in the backyard of his house back in Healdsburg.

After a few minutes of waiting, Vector showed up, walking in with a sour look on his face. He scowled when he saw Connor and the guards around the room. When he recognized the general, he saluted.

"Is this a hologram?" Vector asked, looking at the man.

"It is not, Private. You have been summoned here as a

sparring partner for conscript Pereira. The rules of the match are Melee only," Major Sanders said sternly.

The adults in the room stood back against the walls as Connor took position opposite Vector, falling into a fighting stance. Vector laughed as he produced a long spear from his OMBI.

"I hope I don't hurt you too bad, kid," Vector said sarcastically.

"Good luck getting me when I have both arms working," Connor retorted, focusing on the older boy in front of him.

"Begin," Harruhama said loudly.

Connor moved first, running at an angle toward Vector's left side. Vector rotated, stabbing forward at his opponent.

Connor dropped to his knees, sliding forward under the spear thrust, coming in close. He grabbed the spear with one hand and lifted himself off the ground, throwing a kick toward Vector's knee. The spear dissipated in Connor's hand, throwing his balance off as Vector came in hard, suddenly holding a short sword and shield.

Connor fell back, dodging sword swings by twisting his body and rolling backwards across the mat. It occurred to Connor that with virtual weaponry he probably couldn't deflect real sword swipes, and certainly not with his bare hands.

Vector pushed forward, trying to corner the smaller boy to finish the match quickly. Connor continued his twisting and rolling, moving just ahead of the blade before it cut him. When he neared the corner, he feigned right but rolled left under a heavy swing. Coming up behind Vector, Connor launched a series of punches that landed upon solid metal. He had almost disabled Vector but the boy raised his armor plating too quickly.

Now, fully armored, Vector continued his approach against Connor, altering his weapon into a long chain with a spiked head at the end. The weapon whirled around above Vector's head teasingly.

"You're going to need to hit me harder than that, kid," Vector taunted.

Connor knew this fight was going to be difficult, but watching a heavily armored, larger opponent moving his direction, he was beginning to wonder if it was impossible.

"Not impossible," he heard a whisper say inside his head.

He felt a sense of calm come over him as he watched Vector move. The older boy was acting aggressively and foolishly, over-extending himself trying to end the match as quickly as he could. Connor realized that Vector was relying heavily on his armor to protect him and leaving himself vulnerable in a lot of areas.

Connor took a deep breath, closing his eyes and imaging the outcome he desired: beating Vector into the infirmary.

—

Seeing the arrogent little hisser stop and close his eyes, Vector heaved the heavy spiked ball around into a wide arc that would catch the twerp on the side of his head. As the ball spun toward his opponent, Connor's eyes popped open and he took two quick steps forward. Connor grabbed at the chain and threw his weight against it, decreasing the radius of the spiked head's arc, before letting go.

Vector couldn't react fast enough as his own weapon slammed heavily into his chest, staggering him back. Connor was on him in an instant; off-balance and disoriented, Vector felt the kid grab onto his back and kick out the back of his knees. Vector fell hard to the ground on his back, the wind forced from his lungs, his arm pulled tightly to the side as he tried to orient himself. He looked over as Connor was frantically cycling through the menus on his OMBI. Vector blinked a couple of times and looked again, realizing that it wasn't Connor's OMBI, but his own. He felt his armor dissipate from his body and the rain of fists that followed. Connor stood above him, punching out as hard as he could.

It occurred to Vector that he should be seizing up, stunned by Connor's attacks, but he wasn't. Then it hit him, the kid had turned off his own OMBI's fist weapon so the fight wouldn't end.

He felt a foot snap his rib with the weight of a heavy jump behind it. Connor moved over to his arm, stomping on his wrist. Vector tried to reactivate his armor with his neuro-sync, but couldn't focus at all with the amount of pain the younger boy was inflicting upon him. He felt something hit hard against the side of his head, and then the whole world went dark.

—

When Vector's body went limp, Connor stopped punching. He stood up after a moment and let out a loud yell, the frustration of his time in the infirmary being released in a primal moment of victory.

Everyone in the room was stunned as Connor walked toward General Harruhama. The man even subconsciously took a step backwards into the wall as the boy approached.

"He is going to need an AFMR or someone to take him to the infirmary, don't you think?" Connor said, looking at Major Sanders, who was staring back at him with a concerned look on his face.

"Guard, call in an AFMR." Harruhama pointed at a guard near the door.

"Well, did I perform as expected, General?" Connor asked, wiping his forehead with his sleeve.

"Just as I hoped you would, young man," the general said, smiling at Connor.

—

When they got back into the observation lounge, Colonel Setzer was there waiting for them. He had just finished yelling at the administrator for not informing him immediately of General Harruhama's visit.

The woman was crying when they got off the lift. Connor was the first out the door and greeted her with a huge smile. The woman turned her head away, tears streaming down her face from Setzer's tirade.

"There there, I am sure it wasn't because you completely suck at your job or anything." Connor chuckled as he walked by.

The woman scowled at him as he strolled past her and into the lounge. When Setzer looked up from behind his desk to see Connor walking in smiling, a scowl appeared on his face too.

"What are you doing here, conscript?" the man asked in a threatening tone.

"I told General Harruhama about you trying to have me killed in a training room, and he's here with a firing squad," Connor said with a smirk.

"What?!" Setzer screamed as Harruhama, Sanders, and the twelve guards walked through the door.

Connor sat down in an open seat and watched the man's face turn white.

"Colonel Setzer, I presume?" the general asked.

"I don't know what this kid might have told you, but I didn't have anything to do with the attack. He has made a lot of enemies with that smart attitude of his!" Setzer said frantically.

"Calm down, Colonel. What attack are you talking about?" Harruhama asked patiently.

Setzer looked at Connor with an angry glare to see the boy smiling back at him, on the verge of laughter.

"Oh it's nothing, General. Some boys got into a fight in a

training room and Pereira ended up in the infirmary for a few days," Setzer said, backpedaling.

"I trust a full investigation was made and the perpetrators punished?" Harruhama asked.

"Of course," was all the man said.

"I'm sure the general won't mind if you forwarded him your report," Major Sanders cut in, offering Connor a wink.

"Yes, please do, Colonel." Harruhama nodded.

"Of course, sir," Setzer said through gritted teeth.

Connor watched delightedly as the man squirmed. He hadn't expected Major Sanders to step in and help out, but it made him wonder if he should reevaluate his dislike for the man.

"On to business; as you know conscript Pereira has proven a capable and rational commander. We have a special assignment for him if he accepts it."

"Yes, sir." Setzer was still sweating from his bald head.

Harruhama walked over to where Connor was sitting and kneeled down.

"I would like you to come with us to a special training facility, where your skills will be put to use for the greater good of the UEDF."

"Why me?" Connor asked curiously.

"Because we need you to pilot *Hati*. I'm not sure if you know it, but you created a slipstream portal when you went to the Eagle Nebula that carried you much faster than we thought possible," Harruhama explained quietly.

Intrigued, Connor asked, "How much faster?"

"The time lapse for you was twelve hours. The previous record was two-and-a-half weeks at that distance, and the standard slipstream takes months! You saved the lives of all the survivors of the UEDF Griswold with your jump, Connor."

"I had no idea. I was just worried about my brother," Connor said earnestly.

"Will you come with us and help us on a special mission against the Gortha?" Harruhama asked gently.

"Sure, but can I say goodbye to my friends here?" Connor asked, looking like a little boy for the first time since Harruhama had met him.

"Sure, Connor. I have business at the Academy; our transport will leave in twenty-four hours. Go be with your friends."

Connor turned to leave the room, pausing to look back at Colonel Setzer. He raised his fist, pointing one finger at the man, and jerking his hand backwards like he had just pulled a trigger. Then he ran to the lift and back to the Blue Army barracks to say his goodbyes.

CHAPTER 15

An old familiar feeling

H E AWOKE TO THE SMELL OF CINNAMON ROLLS BAKING, the sweet air stirring him from a dream that dissipated ephemerally like smoke in the wind. He opened his eyes and looked around the room. It was a small apartment decorated with pictures of people he didn't recognize. There was no holotube in the room, but an old-style record player was spinning, quietly playing an unfamiliar, haunting instrumental piece.

He was lying on an old couch made from a coarse fabric that held up firmly against the weight of his body. Trying to sit up against the heavy blanket, he felt pain rippling with every movement. He could tell he had been injured, but couldn't remember how. His ankle hurt the worst of all and, fighting the sting, he managed to sit upright. When he went to remove the blanket from his body, he realized he wasn't wearing any clothes. Modesty set in and he sat back, trying to remember how he got there.

He couldn't. He couldn't remember anything at all.

The sound of somebody moving in the next room caused him to reach unconsciously for a weapon on his back that was not there.

"Now why'd I do that?" he asked to himself.

"Oh, you're awake!" a woman's voice said from the next room.

A woman wearing a light-blue dress walked through the doorway, carrying a tray of cinnamon rolls. She was a mature woman, in her mid-50s maybe with dark-brown eyes and light-blonde hair that was beginning to show the edges of gray on her temples. When she smiled at him, deep lines of a stress-filled life creased around her eyes. She had an aura of gentleness that made her seem like she had raised children and carried herself like a woman who was not afraid.

"Hi," he said, trying to smile against the pain of his body.

"Hello, I'm April," She greeted warmly. "Who might you be sir?"

"I am not really sure; I mean, I can't remember exactly." He fought against the haze in his mind to try to remember his own name.

"I see. Well, you hit your head plenty hard out there; give it a few minutes and see how you feel. I managed to drag you inside and treat your wounds. They looked pretty bad."

She walked around to the couch and pulled up his blanket, examining his foot. From a nearby end table she grabbed a jar and began spreading a cool cream on his injury.

"Thank you for helping me," he said earnestly. "What is that?"

"It's a poultice to reduce swelling. I think you broke your ankle." She grimaced as she worked.

"Do you know what happened to me?" he asked, feeling the pain relieve in his foot a bit.

"Well. I found you near the airport under a bridge. A bright white light caused me to look outside my window and the whole area exploded. When I went outside, I found you lying there, alive. Since the riots started, I haven't been able to get a hold of emergency services, so I took you in."

"Thank you kindly, April." He smiled as he rested back against the cushion.

"Would you like a cinnamon roll? You've been out for days, I'm sure you're hungry."

"That would be great."

He grabbed one of the hot rolls and broke it apart with his fingers, putting a small piece in his mouth. The cinnemon roll was delicious, igniting his taste buds.

"Connor would love these," he remarked offhandedly. The name was fuzzy in his mind and in an instant, was gone. "Who's Connor?"

"Sorry, I have no idea," April replied, going back into the kitchen. She returned moments later with a tall glass of milk.

"You're too kind. Really, thank you," he said, taking a drink of the milk.

She smiled at him and sat down on a chair next to the couch, watching him eat.

"Marlena, do you know where my clothes are?" he asked, remembering that he was naked under the blanket.

"It's April dear. I have them hanging out to dry right now. They were an absolute mess when I found them."

"I'm sorry, April. What did I say?"

"You called me Marlena. Is that someone you know?"

The thumb on his left hand unconsciously moved to stroke the gold wedding band he wore.

"Maybe … I think she is my wife," He replied, fighting to remember.

"Could very well be; although, I'm not sure what kind of a wife would leave her handsome husband alone on the street, near death." April flashed him another smile.

He smiled back uncertainly while grabbing another cinnamon roll off the tray and eating it. The smell made him think of a kitchen he used to bake in with his family. Their faces were shadows in the memory and he couldn't quite place where they were supposed to be.

"I think my memory is starting to come back. I can remember a house in a valley surrounded by vineyards," he said to her, trying hard to piece together the images in his head.

"Sounds lovely, but there aren't any places like that around here."

"Where is 'here'?" he asked.

"Queens, New York."

"Oh. You mentioned something about a riot, is it dangerous around here?"

"It's not so bad in Queens. Manhattan is completely closed off and surrounded; a lot of other places are too. Things are getting bad everywhere these days."

"Wow. What happened?"

"Oh, a terrorist killed two members of the Earth Military Council and started a global conspiracy, which caused everyone to go nuts. I don't know why though, the UEDF always seemed pretty good to me." April shrugged.

"Well, what about..." he began.

She interrupted him, saying, "I think that's enough talk about that for now, why don't you rest a bit. You were almost dead two days ago, after all."

"Okay. Thanks again for helping me."

He rested back under the blanket and drifted to sleep.

———

He knew it was a dream before he heard her footsteps in the hall. This house no longer existed. He remembered that explosion, even in his sleep. It had been hard to make the decision to sacrifice his entire estate; he had taken so much pride in building it with his family. He'd set the explosives, knowing full well that they might kill him, and timed the egress into the safe room behind the bookshelf in his office, when the operative ran out. He even thought he timed it right so that the assassin wouldn't escape.

Her smile disrupted the disturbing memories of the day he faked his death. Her red lips curving upwards, promising a sweet escape from the stress of his memories. She peeked into the office with a playful look in her eye. From behind the door, she raised a bottle of wine and two glasses.

"It's just you and me tonight," she said, her lips forming each word carefully. Her dark hair swayed as she leaned into the room, coming around the corner wearing a red dress.

"You look beautiful, Mrs. Mercer," William said, a smile forming on his face.

"And you look very handsome, Mr. Mercer." She walked up to him, looking up at him with her almond-colored eyes.

He grabbed her around her waist and pulled her close. He could smell the scent of melon in her hair as he breathed in deep, intoxicated by this woman.

"Why, sir, whatever are you doing?" she said playfully, twirling her hair with her left hand.

"I am loving you with all my heart, Marlena." The sincere weight of his tone caused her to shiver.

"I got chills."

Tears rimmed his dark-blue eyes. "I did too. I wish this weren't a dream."

"Me too, baby. I miss you."

"I miss you too, every day," he said as his tears began to fall.

⁓

William awoke in the darkness, tears in his eyes as he sat up against the pain of his injuries. His memory had come back in his sleep and he knew he couldn't stay in this place any longer.

"April, are you there?" he called into the darkness.

After a moment, a light came on from a room off the kitchen.

"What's the trouble, dear?" she asked, coming into the room wearing a long robe.

"I'm sorry, but I have to leave."

"You're in no condition to go anywhere. Why don't you rest?" She sat on the chair next to the couch.

"I appreciate all you have done for me, truly. But I am putting you in danger by being here and I need to go."

"I find that hard to believe, how am I in any danger?" she asked, sounding confused.

"Because I am the Dragoon, the terrorist who started the riots, the riots that are becoming a revolution and I am a prime target for UEDF troops."

"I see. Are you going to kill me?" she asked quietly.

"Of course not," he replied, trying to sound unthreatening.

She stared at him for a long while before speaking again.

"It's a shame."

"Sorry?"

"It's nothing, I'll get you your things. But you are going to have trouble walking on that ankle for a while," April warned as she went into the next room.

"I know it. I'll manage though."

She walked back in a minute later dragging his mechanized battle armor and clothes behind her. She set them by the couch and left the room.

He slowly got dressed into his battle armor, which fit tightly against his skin, causing his aches to flare up. He grimaced as he bent over to put his pants on over the suit and proceeded to get dressed through the pain. He could barely put any weight on his ankle, even with the battle armor enhancing his movements.

April came back in carrying his hat and gun. She handed the objects to him and moved in close, hugging him. William

Mercer stood there holding his hat and weapon, accepting the hug passively.

"You seem like a good man. Be careful out there," she said, letting him go.

William pulled his bandana up around his face and put his large-brimmed hat onto his head. He tipped the edge of the hat toward the woman who had saved his life.

"Thank you again, for saving my life."

Using his gun as a makeshift walking stick, the man hobbled out of the apartment.

—

When he got down to the street level, all was quiet. The sky had a pale orange color to it and the air was cool as he exited the apartment building. He had no idea how long he'd slept in April's apartment or even what time it was, but it was clearly late. The fires set from the attempt on his life had been out for a long time. He walked slowly in the direction of what used to be JFK Airport, taking heavy steps that sent ripples of pain shooting through his legs.

He knew he wouldn't make it too far walking, but hoped that as soon as he could get into the military transport station, he might find an AMFR or at least some pain medication. The UEDF IG soldiers hadn't rebuilt the checkpoint since the bombardment and he walked through, finding only ashen remains of what used to be a squad of soldiers.

On the far side of the checkpoint William got lucky and discovered an AX-11 utility vehicle that had not been destroyed by the orbital defense cannon. He got inside and searched around for the keys. As luck would have it, the keys were above the visor on the driver's side of the AX-11 and he started it up, listening to the engine grumble for a moment before putting it in gear.

He drove slowly toward the airport, fighting to remain conscious through the waves of agony that were throbbing through his body. The walk to the checkpoint hadn't been long, but the effort on the ruined body of the man had nearly put him on the ground. Now that he was sitting, he had trouble remaining focused and feared that he wouldn't make the short journey to the transport station.

Ahead in the darkness, he could see lights of transports flying in and out of the airport but saw no guards or patrols.

"I guess now that I am dead again, they don't feel so worried all the way over here," he smirked.

He stopped the truck outside the front of a terminal and hobbled into the building as quickly as he could manage. The area wasn't busy at this hour; a few flight mechanics were sitting together drinking coffee at a table on the other side of the terminal and the occasional soldier walked by in a hurry to get somewhere.

He removed his hat and bandana, trying to not seem too obvious as he walked across the terminal, limping heavily. He held his weapon under his duster, trying to keep it out of sight as well. The people here didn't seem overly alert as he proceeded out to the gates. From the windows he saw many VS91 Transport Shuttles and old-fashioned planes at the gates and on the runways. They had brought several battalions into the city in order to quarantine Manhattan and quell the riots, but it looked like the soldiers who had come through were long since gone.

William walked through one of the gates out to the transport. He went straight to the first aid kit in the back of the vehicle, opening it to find some mild pain medication. He consumed six tablets and settled into a seat near the back. He didn't know how to fly an aircraft, unfortunately, and got it in his mind to wait until a pilot arrived. The seat was comfortable and the man closed his eyes, waiting.

He awoke to the sound of someone walking into the VS91. Whoever it was seemed to be alone. In his haze, William hadn't considered how he was going to fight if more than one person arrived to operate the transport. The sun had risen outside and the morning was hazy from the smoke of fires he couldn't see. As the man settled into the cockpit, William waited quietly in the back. The shuttle began to lift off, heading south along the shoreline.

William waited until they were far from the city before walking up to the cockpit and sitting down in the co-pilot chair.

"Hi," he remarked casually.

"What the?!" the pilot said, startled. "Where did you come from?"

"I was in the back, waiting for you. I want to get to the Ombicademy," William said, raising his weapon at the pilot.

"Calm down. If you could fly, you would have, so you're not going to shoot me."

"You're probably right. But you should know that I am the Dragoon, which means I will be killed if you land me anywhere near a base, so really I have nothing to lose."

The cold look in the man's eyes told the pilot he was telling the truth. He looked out the front window for a moment and then turned back toward the man with the strange three-barreled gun pointed at him.

"Okay, Ombicademy it is! Which way?"

"It's off the coast of Japan, on an island called Kita-Daito. Can this transport make it that far?"

"Sure, but I don't know if we will get shot down before we get there," the pilot said, turning the craft northward.

"What's your name?" William asked.

"Captain Blackwell," the pilot replied.

"Well Captain, let's make sure we don't get shot down," William smiled, the comment earning him a glare.

They flew quietly for several hours, William taking pain medication periodically through the flight. Captain Blackwell looked worried for a while but eventually calmed down. After a while, they started talking again.

"I've heard about the Free Man Revolution, that's what they're calling it right? I actually think the current administration needs an overhaul," the pilot said suddenly.

"Free Man Revolution, huh? I like that," William said with a smirk.

"You didn't come up with it?"

"Nope, this is the first I've heard of it. I was just trying to get a little payback."

"Payback for what?"

"The EMC killed someone special to me."

"So this is some kind of quest for vengeance?" the pilot asked curiously.

"It's a reckoning. The EMC invented an alien threat to enslave us and the colonies so that they could remain in power."

"But they were trying to get resources for the people; they wanted to give us energy and food. Without the colonies, the Earth will fall and the people will die."

"So the ends justify the means? How many people have to be murdered and enslaved for this greater good? Who determines what is good? Right now it is a despot who seized power from a democratically elected government with a false flag attack. He murdered a woman for that control."

"When you put it that way it seems pretty obvious, but knowing that many more will die if you win, it's hard to say what's right," Blackwell offered, sounding somewhat sympathetic.

"The difference is, if I win, the only people who will die

are the people who don't earn what they consume. The people waiting for their handout will not make it. Those who want to work, can get to a colony that will accept them, or rebuild this planet will be fine. Just because we exhausted some of the resources on this planet doesn't mean that there aren't an abundance of others that we can't use," William explained.

"If the EMC has their way, they will exhaust the people who produce, whether here or on a colony. Without them, the people waiting for the handout still die. It just takes a little longer. The reasons the colonies are productive and the Earth is not, is because the producers went out there, looking for their chance to live without an oppressive regime stealing the product of their labor. The Earth doesn't have enough producers to accommodate all the consumers," William finished thoughtfully.

Captain Blackwell was quiet for a long time after that, thinking over what William had said. He noticed a bit later that William had passed out and left him alone while he flew the transport toward the Ombicademy. He knew he could have landed and escaped, but found himself agreeing with the man and by the time they were over Japan, he considered himself a Free Man.

"Wake up, we're nearly there." Blackwell nudged William.

"How long was I asleep?" William asked, yawning.

"About four hours. You must be in a lot of pain."

"It's nothing."

"Right," Blackwell said skeptically. "Why do you even want to go to the Ombicademy?"

"They have my son there, and I am going to get him out."

"If they knew who you were, they would have used him a long time ago. He might be safer there than somewhere else in the world," Blackwell said convincingly.

"You're probably right; only, it's just a matter of time

before I'm identified. I need to get my boy out before that happens."

"I will wait on the landing pad, if you want," the pilot offered with a smile.

"I appreciate that," William said as he finished the bottle of pain pills.

"By the way, my name is Jared." The pilot extended his hand.

"I am the Dragoon," William replied back, taking the man's hand.

CHAPTER 16

Crux of a moment

WILLIAM WALKED SLOWLY ACROSS THE RUNWAY, past several transports on his way toward the entrance of the Ombicademy. He leaned heavily on his weapon now, unsure if he would be able to put any weight on his right foot. When he tried he felt waves of pain shooting through his body so intensely that black spots began to cloud his vision.

The tarmac was empty in the middle of the day, and the man was grateful for it. He wasn't sure he would be able to sneak around or fight in his condition. Getting an idea, William went aboard one of the other transports on the deck and into the back where the medical kit was. He found it easily enough and removed the pain medication, consuming a few of the bitter pills right then.

He took a deep breath to steady himself, knowing that he couldn't continue like this for very long. As the medication took effect, the pain began to slightly alleviate. He exited the transport and continued to make his way toward the entrance.

When he finally crossed the runway, William felt exhausted. Moving while heavily injured was taxing his energy; to make matters worse, when he arrived at the doorway, it was sealed shut. He had hoped to avoid discharging his weapon, as to not draw attention to himself, but he didn't see an alternative entrance anywhere nearby and knew that searching around could cost him his consciousness.

From the under-barrel he released a small stream of thermite discs, which spun through the air like a line of blue fire. When they impacted the handle, they began to melt and sizzle. The man watched as the thermite discs attempted to eat away the metal, eventually falling to the ground. The door was undamaged. The man cursed quietly, angry that he didn't have the capability to inflict damage on the strange metal that made up the Ombicademy.

Getting an idea, William slammed the butt of his shotgun against the door twice and stood to the right side. He waited while someone on the other side unlocked the mechanism and stepped through the portal. The airman guarding the door walked outside and was met by the swinging butt of a three-barreled shotgun.

Straining with the effort, William dragged the man to one side and found a small keycard, which the man had apparently used to unlock the door. He moved slowly into the structure, unsure of which way to proceed. He realized quickly that his outfit would be more likely to give him away than his heavy limp, but without access to an AFMR and a disguise, he decided he would try to be as cautious as he could.

In the middle of the day, there weren't many people around. The occasional conscript walked by, far down the hallway in a hurry to get somewhere. No other airmen or staff were present as he made his way through the unmarked halls of the Ombicademy. He began to grow frustrated, knowing he was close to his stepson, but unsure of how to find him.

He tried several doors he passed with the keycard he'd taken, but none of them opened for him. He was beginning to wonder if it was a keycard at all, but elected to hold on to it. Even if it only opened the exit for him, it would be valuable enough to keep.

After a few minutes he came upon a door that was marked with a large green serpent. The plaque on the wall clearly labeled this as the Green Army barracks. William steadied his resolve, knowing that he was at least on the right level. He toyed with the idea of trying to capture one of the students to get information on where the Blue Army barracks were, but he dismissed the idea, realizing that stealth was a greater ally than information for the time being.

As quietly as he could, he moved through the cold metal corridors in search of Connor.

⁓

"I will write, I promise," Connor said to Cat, who was already crying.

"You better! I can't believe you're already leaving. We were supposed to be here for six years!" she said, her voice still shaken with the news that he was leaving.

Connor had returned to the Blue Army barracks as quickly as he could the day before, telling everyone that he was going on a special assignment with General Harruhama, and that he wouldn't be back for a while. All of his friends were upset by the news. Connor was more than a friend to the soldiers of Blue Army; he was a leader to them, an icon of what they hoped they could be someday.

"I don't think it's forever, I just need to help them escort some ships or something. They really didn't tell me much," Connor offered, shrugging.

"Probably because they knew you would tell everybody." Jinn "Katana" Matsui laughed from his bunk nearby.

"Ha! You're probably right." Connor chuckled.

Cat had been sitting on his bed next to him, holding his hand and weeping. She'd cried when he told her that he was leaving the day before, cried all night, and was crying again now that it was time to go.

"It will be okay, Cat. I'm sure you guys will do fine without me," Connor said, trying to make her feel better.

"If you're stupid enough to think that I'm upset because we might lose fights without you then I ought to smack you until you get it!" she snapped.

Connor looked over at the other boys in Blue Army, who all looked away quickly. He wondered if he would ever understand girls.

When Harruhama's guard showed up and walked into their barracks, Connor stood up off the bed.

"It's time for me to go."

Cat threw her arms around him in a big hug then locked her arm with his as he walked out of the barracks. Ladder and Carl both gave Connor a hug on his way out. Katana, Hunter, and Dice shook his hand and wished him the best. Manzar was crying in his bunk and waved goodbye from there. Even Skulls seemed despondent at the idea of Connor leaving, but got up to pat him on the back on the way out the door.

"Give them hell out there, Commander," Skulls said, saluting.

"I will," Connor replied, putting his hand on his friend's shoulder before continuing on.

When they got to the Guard he looked from Connor to Cat slowly with a stern look on his face.

"She's just going to walk me to the exit, is that okay?"

"Fine," the guard said, seeming sympathetic.

Connor turned at the exit and waved goodbye one final time to Blue Army as he walked out the door.

—

William had found a door he could open, and was glad when he discovered that he was in the infirmary. A 311AFMR was working on an older boy and four other beds were occupied by younger kids in red uniforms. He thought he recognized one of the kids as one of Connor's friends from home, but dismissed it quickly, not wanting to get distracted.

The room was quiet but for the AFMR working. When he began to look through the supply cabinet the robot stopped its work and turned toward him.

"Something AFMR can assist you with?" it asked in a static-laden robotic voice.

"I have a broken ankle; I could use some pain medication or a brace," he said quietly, not wanting to awaken the sedated patients.

The AFMR moved over to an open bed, where the man sat down. He didn't know it, of course, for he had no way of knowing it, but he sat on the very bed where his stepson had laid not two days before, recovering from his injuries. He rested back against the pillow while the medical robot removed his shoe and examined his ankle.

A green light shot out of the thing's single lens, crossing back and forth over the foot. The AFMR used its three arms to stabilize and grip the foot around the edges.

"Prognosis: dislocated ankle set improperly. Setting ankle," the machine warned as it tugged hard on his foot.

William felt waves of pain roll through his body as he clenched his teeth, fighting to remain conscious. The pain medication he had recently taken helped, but even so it was the second worse pain he'd ever felt in his life.

He was breathing heavily and sweating when the AFMR plunged a heavy needle into his foot.

"Ow! What is that?" He growled.

"Synthetic bonding agent," the robot replied mechanically.

As the cool white paste flowed through the needle into his foot, he felt it solidify around in his ankle. The AFRM plunged a second needle, which filled his foot with a green fluid.

"And that?" he asked, grimacing.

"Anti-inflammatory medicine."

When it was over, the AFMR wrapped the foot with several tight bandages, which solidified when the machine sprayed a light film of brown fluid over it. In ten minutes he felt like he could run again if he had wanted to.

"Please rest the foot for forty-eight hours," the AFMR instructed as William put his boot back on.

It went back to work on the other patients as he sat up. William felt much better and could actually put weight on his foot. He knew that he would have to be careful, since the bone solution didn't solidify entirely, but he couldn't waste any more time. As he neared the exit, he heard a voice from behind him.

"Hey, who are you?" asked the baritone voice of the boy on the last bed in the infirmary.

"You're injured, kid; I am just a figment of your imagination," William said, hoping that the kid would just accept it and go back to sleep.

"Huh," the boy said, lying back against his pillow.

—

The guard led Connor and Cat back to the lift, where General Harruhama was waiting for them. He eyed Cat, who was grabbing tightly to Connor's arm, and then looked at the guard.

The man shrugged and said, "She just wants to walk him out."

"I see," Harruhama said slowly. "What is your name, conscript?"

"Amanda McTaggart, sir. I just wanted to see my friend off, if that's okay," she pleaded.

"I am General Harruhama; it's nice to meet you. You can walk us to the exit, but once we're outside you have to go back to your barracks, do you understand?"

"Yes sir, General," Cat said quickly, not wanting to ruin her last few minutes with Connor.

"Thank you," Connor said to him too, as he leaned slightly into Cat.

He wasn't exactly afraid of where he was going, but he knew he would miss his friends when he got there. Cat had become very special to him for reasons he didn't quite understand, but he wanted her to walk with him.

The guards formed up around them, six in front and six behind as they proceeded slowly to the exit of the Academy. Connor hated the idea of leaving, but he sincerely believed he would be back after his mission. He almost asked Harruhama before thinking better of it. If he was wrong, he didn't want to worry Cat at all.

The heavy boots echoed down the corridors as Connor left behind the Ombicademy and the friends who had made it feel like home.

⁓

The sounds of heavy boots in the next hallway over caused the man to freeze. He hadn't seen or heard anyone who sounded like an adult since the airman he disabled on his way in. The children could be convinced that he belonged there, he hoped, but any adult would know he was out of place.

When the echoes had faded, he turned to go. He nearly walked into a man turning around a corner and found himself looking into the wolfish face of Major Edmond Sanders. The major's jaw dropped as he looked back into the cold eyes of the man responsible for starting the Free Man Revolution.

With his left hand, the Dragoon removed his bandana and enjoyed the look of deeper shock that befell Sanders when he realized the man was William Mercer.

"I told you I would make you pay for an eternity," William said coolly as the major looked up and down the halls.

"Follow me!" Sanders said quickly, surprising William by pulling him into a side hall.

The major had been shocked for only a moment, but now was moving with purpose. He hadn't tried to sound an alarm or call out, so William followed him, curious what this man's intention was.

They stopped in the hall, Sanders wheeling about to face William directly.

"You're alive, twice over," Sanders said matter-of-factly.

"Very observant of you," William replied smugly.

"Listen, I have a million things to say but not enough time to say them. You have to get moving right now! Harruhama has taken your son and is going to order an all-out war against Aeris VII. They aren't gone yet, but you are missing your chance. Kill Harruhama if you can; if he dies, this war will end."

"You are a sympathizer?" William asked even as he turned to move.

"Far more than I can say right now. Go!" Sanders said, turning the other direction back toward the lift.

William's head was spinning as he ran through the halls.

He could feel the weight of his body in his injured foot but pushed forward as swiftly as he could. He had known that the Gortha weren't real and that the EMC along with Harruhama were trying to enslave the colonies, but a war? The thought that the colonies were resisting gave him a measure of hope.

He ran like a man possessed, determined to get to his stepson. The idea that his rebellion on Earth could be a second front to a war in space gave him an optimistic view that his adopted sons might know freedom in his lifetime. The thought drove him forward.

He came around the corner to the entrance he had used when he arrived and almost walked right into the barrage of bullets that filled the hallway.

—

Having discovered the unconscious body of the airman door guard, Harruhama ordered Cat down a side hall back to her barracks against her protest. He positioned six guards in the corridor whose orders were to wait until he had gone and then seek out and eliminate the intruder.

The man, the boy, and the other six guards proceeded out onto the tarmac to their transport. They had almost boarded when the open doorway of the Ombicademy erupted with an explosion. The bodies of the guards scattered as they were flung from their defensive positions.

The pilot of Harruhama's transport had the engines firing when the Dragoon appeared from the smoky portal.

He walked with a slight limp toward the transport, firing a barrage of explosive pellets at a guard, who hopped off the transport to stop him. The guard collapsed in a lump as the man moved forward.

"Get us in the air," Harruhama said coldly to the pilot, who was nodding furiously.

He could see that Connor was scared while he grabbed him by the arm, walking toward the exit of the transport. He held Connor over the threshold, watching the man outside reloading his weapon.

"You are a worthy antagonist. But will the Dragoon murder an innocent child?" Harruhama yelled to the man over the sound of the transport engines.

The Dragoon lowered his weapon when he saw Connor.

"I didn't think so!" Harruhama yelled as the transport lifted off the deck, high into the air.

—

William watched with a deep sense of frustration and anger as his stepson departed with the man responsible for the death of his wife. He'd wanted to kill Harruhama, wanted to rescue the boy, but even as he stood there watching the opportunity pass, the man's head begin to whirl with ideas. He knew he would have to kill General Harruhama.

He almost turned to go back inside of the Academy to get information on where Connor had gone, but the sound of an alarm broke his concentration. He looked back to the open doorway and saw a pretty, red-headed young girl staring back at him.

"You didn't stop them!" she cried from the doorway.

"I couldn't get there on time. But I won't give up," he called back.

"You're the Dragoon, right, the man who is setting the world free?" she asked from behind her green, teary eyes.

"I am, but I don't know about setting the world free," he

responded quickly, knowing that he was going to have to run soon.

"Connor said you were. He told us that you were going to win, too."

Tears rimmed his dark-blue eyes. "If you know Connor, then you must be Amanda, right?"

"How did you know that?" She took a stunned step back inside.

"It is nice to meet you, young lady. I'm William Mercer, Connor's stepfather." He tipped his hat and removing his bandana for a moment.

She was clearly shocked by this news. The sound of guards moving down the hallway broke the trance.

"You have to run! Connor has to know that you're alive!" she yelled as she ran back inside.

He was smiling despite himself. He turned to run for the transport on the far side of the runway as the sound of guards neared the doorway. He reached the transport as the armed men began to burst forth, running toward him. The transport lifted off before they got anywhere close to the end of the runway. Captain Blackwell had clearly seen the events unfolding outside and had been prepared to leave at a moment's notice.

When William got on board, Jared turned to him and spoke.

"Was that your son they took?" he asked, seeming to know the answer.

William settled down into the co-pilot seat. "Yes."

"Who was the little girl?"

"That was my son's girlfriend," he said with a smile, despite the gravity of the situation.

Jared shared the grin for a moment before continuing, "So where to, boss?"

"Can you follow that other transport?"

"I don't think so. It left in a hurry, and I don't have that kind of tracking equipment onboard."

"Damn," William growled. "Do you have any idea where they would take him?"

"I can't say. Someone in the Ombicademy might know?" Blackwell offered. "But we're not going to be able to go back that way anytime soon."

William could see other craft beginning to launch from the platforms and as much as it hurt to let Connor go, he was out of options.

"Did we miss our only chance?" William asked, more to himself than to Captain Blackwell.

"For now we did. I am getting us out of here."

"Where to?" William asked

"Well, where does the revolution need the most help?"

"Let's scan the network and find out," William said, putting on a headset.

They flew in the direction that Harruhama had gone for a while, but without seeing the faster transport or having any way to track them, they eventually turned their attention to the growing number of reports of fighting all over the world. Despite wanting to look for his son, William knew that it was hopeless and, for now, his revolution needed him.

—

Eight thousand light years away, Alex stood in front of the Cerulean Sky Café, saying his goodbyes to Lyria. Marlena had flown *Tizona* into the city, landing on a high rooftop with *Skoll* in the cargo hold. She and Alex took a lift down to the street, where she informed him that she was going to go meet with the commanders of the 3rd and 5th fleet before they departed.

Alex had run three blocks to the café where Lyria had

been serving lunch to an older couple. When she saw him in the window she ran outside and jumped into his arms.

"I was afraid you wouldn't come," she said whimpered, pulling herself close to him.

"I had to. I only have a few minutes, but I had to come say goodbye." He put his arms around her.

"You will be gone for five weeks, right?"

"I hope that's all it takes. But if we beat the returning ships by too much, it may be longer. It's hard to say just how long a slipstream will take," he explained as he moved his hands up and down her back.

"You know, you keep traveling that way and I am going to be a lot older than you someday," she said with a grin.

"Well, I shouldn't have to do it much longer if we can find a way to stop the war," he replied, sharing her grin.

"I know you will. I believe in you." Lyria kissed Alex's cheek softly.

His face flushed a deep crimson as he replied, "Then I guess I will have to."

The two shared another kiss before they parted. Alex met his mom at the base of the building and proceeded back onto the lift to the rooftop.

"How did it go?" she asked him.

"Good," Alex replied, looking distant.

"The commanders are ordering the fleets back to protect Aeris, so she should be safe until we get back," Marlena offered.

"Good," he replied again, a little more enthusiastically.

The two shared a smile as Marlena put her hand on her son's back. As they exited the lift and boarded the *Tizona*, Alex paused to look back over the planet he had come to love.

"It's really great here," he said to her, closing the cargo bay doors.

"That's why we have to protect it," she replied, moving through the cargo bay up to the flight deck.

"Hey, since we're going to miss it in slipstream, happy birthday, Mom," Alex called up to a smiling Marlena.

—

From behind a crate in the cargo hold, Operative One heard the comment too and smiled. He knew he would have to bide his time with the dangerous boy on board, but he was trained to be patient, and so he waited quietly as the engines of the *Tizona* ignited, lifting them high into the sky.

CHAPTER 17

A long way down

T HE FLIGHT ON THE TRANSPORT WAS SPENT IN SILENCE, Connor staring out the window at the ocean below, thinking about what he had just seen. The Dragoon was at the Ombicademy, coming after Harruhama! The thought didn't sit right with the boy, since Harruhama had only been on the island for a short time. Surely this man hadn't anticipated him right to that moment.

Then what? Connor's mind swirled furiously, trying to come up with the answer. Was the man after him? That even made less sense to Connor.

Harruhama was shouting orders through a communicator while Connor listened. He was trying to organize a search for the man, who had been declared dead forty-eight hours before. He listened to the old general screaming at someone on the other end of the transmission, glad he was not that person.

The fight at the academy had made Connor wonder if his friends were okay, until he heard Harruhama yelling about how the man escaped.

After a couple of hours the old man seemed to settle down, speaking calmly, issuing orders to various parts of the world. Apparently there were a lot of battles going on across the globe and Connor wondered how bad it was. He figured the Ombicademy was safe now, since the Dragoon left and he didn't have any friends anywhere else, so he didn't let it affect him too much.

"How bad is it?" Connor asked when Harruhama set down his headset.

"That's nothing that a ten-year-old boy should worry about. We have other matters to attend to," the man said cryptically.

"It's just that, I have two uncles in Florida and Argentina, and I was wondering how bad the riots had gotten there."

"I see. Most of the damage is in the major cities; the more rural areas don't have a lot of UEDF bases, so even if the citizens were angry, they wouldn't have anyone to attack."

"Is it going to be okay though?" Connor asked seriously.

"The lies that the Dragoon has spread have hurt us, but we will make it right," Harruhama stated, trying to dismiss the subject.

"What lies?" Connor asked innocently.

Harruhama knew enough to keep his mouth shut. To even hint to the boy that he had ordered his mother to be murdered would undermine this entire operation. For a moment, he considered aborting the plan all together.

"Never mind; we have a lot of work to do ahead, you should focus on that." The general picked his headphones back up.

Connor didn't appreciate being dismissed so casually one bit. He accessed his OMBI and unlocked the *Neuro-Sync* option. He enjoyed the images of menus in his head that he could scroll through at the speed of thought.

"Now why didn't I do this a long time ago?" he asked to himself quietly.

Connor used the device to reach into the communicator that General Harruhama was using and listened. The man was faking a transmission, meaning he was avoiding the question. He reached out through the ship and found the pilot's cellular communicator, which he used to access the media networks inside his mind.

He dug around until he found the now-sealed file of the Dragoon's presentation in Central Park. He watched the entire thing while staring out the window of the transport. He listened as the presentation told him that the EMC had been responsible for his mother's death.

He felt a familiar heat rising in his chest as his vision turned red. Connor was so mad that he almost attacked Harruhama right in the transport. He took several deep breaths, trying to steady himself, trying to remember William's advice on how to keep calm.

He hadn't followed the advice in the past very much, but sitting there facing five armed guards and the leader of the oppressive militaristic government, he thought he had better remain in control.

Connor cooled his mind and thought about revenge. He'd learned to love that word recently. He knew that it wasn't healthy to pursue vengeance as a manner of living, but lately he knew a lot of people who deserved a little payback.

—

After a couple of hours of seething anger, Connor saw a small metal object out in the water. It looked like a landing pad, but with nothing around it. Slowly the transport circled and landed on the metal pad and the guards began to vacate the craft. Connor got up and followed them outside, where he watched the transport fly back into the sky, leaving them there.

One of the guards got on his communicator and said, "Send the lift."

They waited for several minutes until the tubular glass lift came out of the metal pad. They boarded it and slowly descended into the ocean. Connor looked out the window at the water as the daylight faded above, wondering what sort of special mission he would be getting underwater. As the tube continued downward, Connor eventually saw the lights of a facility below.

When they arrived at the bottom, they disembarked, walking down a long clear hallway toward one of the large domes in the facility.

"Initiator!" Connor heard the voice like a scream in his head.

He'd heard whispers before and knew that he had been getting feedback from his OMBI in the past, but never before had he heard anything scream to him like that.

When the door opened, he saw it: *Hati* kneeling down before him like a seven-winged wolf-knight in white armor paying homage to his lord. Connor nodded toward the machine and smiled, seeing it as a sort of friend, but also as an opportunity.

"I am going to leave you with specialist Larkin, Connor. I will check on your progress in a few days," Harruhama said as he exited the room too quickly.

His opportunity gone for now, Connor turned his attention back on the ship that had taken him across the galaxy.

A man wearing a black uniform walked up and stood next to Connor while he was staring at *Hati*. It was all Connor could do to not board the ship and try to break the glass walls around him.

"So you're the kid who can pilot that, eh?" the man said in a friendly tone.

"I guess so. Have other people tried?" Connor asked, thinking he knew the answer.

"Yeah, we tried. But it doesn't work for us," Larkin said quietly.

"It didn't work for me right away either, I had to trick it." Connor turned to look at the man.

Specialist Larkin was a tall man with sandy-blond hair. He

didn't look like he was much older than Alex except that his light-blue eyes seemed tired.

"How did you do that? With your inhibitor chips in, I mean," Larkin asked, curious.

"Uh, I had to sing. I don't want to talk about it," Connor said, embarrassed. He didn't want Larkin to ask him to "meow" a few songs to try to get *Hati* to move.

"I see. Well, that's no problem. I'm going to remove your inhibitor chips so that you won't have to trick it anymore."

"All of them?" Connor asked hopefully. He had seen what Vector was capable of and enjoyed the idea of being able to produce weapons right then.

"No, just one for today; the first one that makes it so your OMBI only makes weapons in the Ombicademy training rooms and arenas," Larkin explained.

"Then what?" Connor asked.

"Then I am going to let you train on a simulator for a while with another student."

"Who?"

"A kid named Vertigo."

"Oh, I know him! I thought he was dead. He was a friend of my brother!" Connor was excited to be able to get some information on Alex.

"I know. They say you saved his life," Larkin said as he sat Connor down on a chair in the engineering bay.

"When?" Connor asked, confused as Larkin began taking apart the cover of his OMBI.

"When you brought the *Griswold* back from the Eagle Nebula, he was on board."

"Oh. Then I guess he owes me one!" Connor grinned.

His smiled was erased quickly as a wave of nausea came over him. Larkin had removed the face plate and was staring at the OMBI's inhibitor chips intently. The man produced a pair of pliers and proceeded to gently remove the first inhibitor.

Connor felt like he was going to vomit. Dizziness washed over him like he was spinning up through a tornado, twirling high into the sky. Then it was over. When the chip came out, Connor felt immediately better.

As his first order of business, he manifested a Dragunov sniper rifle into his hands. The thing was glowing with a bright-blue light as he gripped it with his left hand.

"So if I shoot someone with a virtual weapon outside the arena, will they still get stunned?" Connor asked curiously.

"I think so; for a little while, anyway," Larkin replied cautiously. "Don't shoot anyone though, kid."

Connor let the weapon dissipate and smiled at the specialist.

"I won't," he said unconvincingly.

"Right," Larkin replied, sounding skeptical, "Let's get you into the simulator, if you're feeling up to it."

"Yeah, I feel fine. Let's go." Connor's words were filled with enthusiasm.

They walked into the corner of the room, where a large white helmet was resting on a table near a black-and-white chair.

Connor sat in the chair as Larkin placed the helmet over his head. It was dark inside the helmet and he could hear Larkin on the outside tapping his fingers against a datapad. Then the scene changed. He was outside on a sandy beach starring at two large Battle Suit Vessels.

"Hey, kid. They told me you were going to be here," the older boy said to him.

Vertigo was sitting on a rock nearby; he looked like he had been waiting for a while.

"You're Austin, right?" Connor asked.

"Call me Vertigo, kid, or Corporal if you're into the whole 'chain of command' thing," Vertigo replied with a grin.

"Sorry. I'm Raptor. You knew my brother, right?"

"Yeah, I did. But I can't talk about it, so don't ask. You ready to get to work?"

Connor wasn't happy with the answer he got, but he turned back toward the Battle Suits and walked over to the smaller one.

It was vaguely the same size as *Hati*, but looked plain compared to the real suit's striking features. The larger suit was huge and made Connor wonder what sort of vessel it was designed after.

Vertigo boarded his vessel by running up the leg and rolling into the cockpit. The battle suit closed around him and stood up.

"I'm going to pull a few maneuvers; see if you can follow."

"What are we preparing for anyway? I don't know anything about the mission."

"Right; as I understand it, there is a Gortha convoy coming toward Earth through a slipstream, and we are going to intercept it," Austin said as his Battle Suit Vessel leapt into the sky, firing its thrusters. After a moment it leveled out, hovering out above the water.

Connor accessed his Neuro-sync and in his mind went through his menus to unlock the suit he was in. He found *Hati* listed on the main menu and was delighted that it was apparently free for him to use. When he unlocked it, a sub-menu came down with many different specialized weapons he could use. He opted to not spend any points on those, since they weren't free.

From his training in the Ombicademy, Connor had learned that the more skilled he got with something, the cheaper it became to unlock as an ability of his OMBI. They'd told him that the device would sync to his brain, but he didn't understand exactly how it all worked.

He climbed on the leg as he had done before and crawled into the cockpit. It felt familiar even in its virtual form. When before he felt at odds with the machine, trying to subconsciously make it move by anticipating motion, now it felt as if it were an extension of his own limbs.

With *Hati* unlocked, Connor fired the thrusters and lifted off the beach into the sky, hovering next to Vertigo.

"Good, kid. Now let's have some fun," Vertigo said over the open communication line.

The larger vessel lifted into the sky and turned out over the water. It spread its large wings and soared down so that it was a few feet above the surf, flying swiftly.

Connor leaned forward, letting his ship tilt until the last moment before firing his thrusters. He reached down as he flew, touching the water. He was amazed that the simulation allowed him to feel through the vessel's hands like they were his own. He caught up to the larger ship quickly, and began flying circles around it.

"You learn fast, Raptor. Ready to take it to the next level?" Vertigo asked, bringing his ship upright.

Large cannons appeared on the shoulders of Vertigo's ship and started firing at *Hati*. He dodged and spun around them easily enough until the larger vessel launched a dozen small missiles at him.

Connor reached through his OMBI and unlocked armor for his right arm, chest, head, and a force barrier for good measure. He liked the idea of using personal unlocks that worked well for his ship too.

He manifested a gun in the ship's large hands, which appeared as a larger version of the 92fs that Connor used in the arena. He turned his ship in midair and began shooting at the targets that Vertigo launched at him. One by one they exploded until twelve missiles became six, then three.

Connor hadn't gotten the last three as they exploded harmlessly against his force field. He let go of his pistol and manifested the large ship version of the Dragunov sniper rifle and took aim at Vertigo's ship, which was now several hundred yards away.

He began firing a stream of bullets, which smacked into the larger vessel's hull, causing it to take some damage before Vertigo put up his own armor and force field. Connor continued to fire as Vertigo angled his ship in Connor's direction. When it got close enough, Connor let go of his sniper rifle and manifested a grenade and pulled the large pin.

He counted as Vertigo came at him, and at the last moment threw the weapon forward as he launched himself into the air. The grenade exploded against Vertigo's force field; the blast disorienting the older boy for a moment. He looked up just in time to see Connor's ship diving downward onto his back.

The smaller vessel's arms punched out furiously in a barrage of heavy strikes that threatened to take down the larger ship's armor. Not to be outdone, Vertigo rolled his ship so that his back was facing the water and dropped slightly. The force of the water pulled *Hati* off.

As the larger ship slowed to turn back around, Connor's ship burst upwards from the water, firing from his handgun once again. The large bullets ricocheted off the vessel's heavy armor.

"I'm impressed, kid. That little ship is pretty agile. But…" Vertigo said into the mic as he manifested a large chain gun.

The gun began to burst out a barrage heavy bullets that rippled across the water and straight toward Connor. The younger boy dodged and flipped, trying to avoid the stream of fire until he could figure out a way to defeat it. A few of the shots would hit his force field and Connor knew that it wouldn't last forever.

Manifesting his fist weapon, Connor spun his ship into broad circles and flew toward Vertigo. As he picked up speed, he dropped below the water and hit his thrusters as hard as he could. Heavy gunfire was still cutting the water around him as he moved away from the deadly barrage, bursting out of the water just below Vertigo's ship.

He came up quickly, punching out hard at the larger ship, trying to grapple it so that it couldn't pull him off. The two ships tussled, Vertigo taking heavy damage from Connor's brutal assault. The chain gun dissipated and the larger vessel manifested a large sword.

The two ships clashed hard, one driving heavy swings of a sword into his opponent, the other landing hit after hit into the body and head. It seemed like they would tear each other apart when the simulation suddenly ended.

Connor was shocked when the helmet came off and he was looking at Specialist Larkin. Larkin was smiling down at him and clapped him on the shoulder.

"Good job, kid!" Larkin said enthusiastically.

"Not that good. He had way more weapons than I do," Connor said, breathing heavily from the effort of the battle.

"The simulation ended with a draw; you took him down too." Larkin laughed.

"I did? Sweet!" Connor said, smiling to himself, for the moment forgetting where he was and feeling like a kid again.

—

For two weeks Connor lived under the ocean, practicing with his ship. Seven days after he had last seen daylight, he awoke early and noticed the date on his OMBI making him sad. July 28th, 2121. It was his mom's birthday. For the last six years, he and William had gone to her grave and placed a bouquet of flowers down in her memory. Not sure of how to honor her this year, Connor asked Larkin for some red paint.

On *Hati's* arm, Connor did his best to paint the image of a

Phoenix along with the date of her death. He missed a practice to finish it, but nobody bothered him.

As the weeks went on, Connor and Austin always flew the same two ships and fought simulated battles against Gortha raiders and capital ships. Sometimes they would fight each other, always ending in a draw. Connor could tell Vertigo was getting frustrated by the battles ending that way, since he was clearly better trained and had far more weapons unlocked.

Connor chalked it up to quick thinking and adaptability; having the more maneuverable ship gave him an advantage that he used as often as he could. Connor wished he could test himself in a training room with Omega on the *Hati*, since he was feeling pretty confident with it. He figured he could earn a ton of points to unlock the various weapons and upgrades, too. Sadly, he assumed since he was in a simulator and not in an Academy training room, he wouldn't get the opportunity to train with the hologram.

Vertigo had treated Connor pretty well during their training sessions, but he never saw the boy in person. He knew that Alex had been friends with the guy, so he figured he could trust him. Although, Alex had left him to die aboard a ruined Battle Frigate, which made Connor wonder if he was right or not.

At the end of the second week of training, General Harruhama came to check on Connor's progress.

"How is he doing, Specialist?" he asked Larkin while Connor was still in the simulator.

"He has excelled at every test we've given him. I think he might have been ready to fight the Gortha on the day he arrived here. He has fought Vertigo to a standstill in every match," Larkin said with a smile on his face.

"Well, they said he was a prodigy. I am glad that it wasn't all talk."

"It really wasn't. Give him a couple years and that ship,"

he said, pointing to *Hati*, "and this kid will be the best pilot the UEDF has ever seen."

"We don't have a couple of years; we have a couple of days. Is he ready now?"

"I believe he is, yes." Larkin's response was confident.

"Then end the simulation," Harruhama said sternly.

Connor felt the simulation end and pulled off the white helmet, turning on Larkin.

"I had him right where I wanted him. I was just about to win!" Connor barked angrily.

"Connor, we have received a report of a Gortha attack vessel coming through a slipstream to the Sol system. We are sending a response team that includes five Battle Frigates, you, and Vertigo," Harruhama said, confirming what Vertigo had told him two weeks prior.

"All that for one ship?" Connor asked doubtingly.

"We don't want to underestimate this enemy, Connor. They have proven to be more resourceful than we would like." Harruhama actually sounded scared to Connor.

"Okay, well, I am ready for it whenever," Connor said dismissively.

Inwardly, Connor was congratulating himself on his excellent acting and fully planned to crush Harruhama the moment they let him back into *Hati*.

CHAPTER 18

A Trick of the Light

As FATE WOULD HAVE IT, HARRUHAMA LEFT THE BASE the night before the mission, leaving for an undisclosed location, before Connor had even woken up.

When he asked Larkin about it, the man shrugged as a reply. Although he was frustrated, Connor knew he would get his chance at Harruhama again, just as soon as he dealt with these Gortha. Every simulation against Gortha ships had Connor and Vertigo winning the fight. They hadn't faced anything that made him think there was anything that could beat him. He even thought that if he got the chance to fight Vertigo again, he would win.

When he awoke the morning of his mission, he was feeling excited. He knew the power of the ship he was about to get back, and was eager to feel it working for him consciously for once.

Larkin was in the engineering dome when Connor walked in.

"Hey, kid, you ready for your big mission?"

"Yeah, piece of cake," Connor said, yawning.

"I have to remove your second inhibitor, so you can manifest weapons in real life. I really mean it, don't shoot anybody!" Larkin warned.

"I won't, I won't. You worry too much, Larkin," Connor

quipped, smiling at the idea of holding real weapons instead of simulated ones.

Connor sat in the chair where Larkin had removed his first inhibitor as the man gathered his tools.

"What do the other two do?" Connor asked him as he began removing the cover plate.

"The third is designed to keep the data transfer between your brain and the OMBI one way, so you can command it without it trying to influence you. The fourth is the inhibitor designed to allow the UEDF access to your information and controls the point system," Larkin explained as he removed the cover plate.

"Wait, why don't you just take them all out then?" Connor asked seriously.

"Because without the third one, your brain could fry, and without the fourth, the UEDF wouldn't be able to tell if you were ready for combat."

Connor began to feel the familiar waves of nausea as Larkin removed the second inhibitor. It was slightly different from the first time, but still felt like he was being spun around in his chair. When the chip was removed Connor looked right into the man's eyes.

"When do I get the others removed?"

"When you're ready, I guess. I have never heard of anyone having more than these two removed," Larkin replied. "Why don't you try to manifest your knife."

Connor concentrated and manifested his knife in his left hand. The blue blade looked sharp and felt very real to the touch.

"Good, kid, you're ready to go!"

Connor got up and walked around, changing his vision from normal to thermal imagining and back again. He felt extremely strong suddenly and realized that he could be a very dangerous person.

He raised and lowered his armor for good measure and

concentrated on the electronics in the room. He could feel them out there, waiting to become his tools if he desired. When he looked at *Hati*, he thought he felt the ship smiling at him.

—

Connor had been wondering how he was going to get *Hati* out of the dome until Larkin informed him there were smaller domes that they could flood. When it was time to launch, Connor thanked the man for helping him. Larkin seemed a little shocked by that, since the kid had seemed meaner than a badger on most occasions. He managed to sputter out a "you're welcome" before sending Connor and *Hati* down a conveyor into a small dome.

The room was empty and not well-lit. Connor sat in the cockpit ready to emerge from the ocean in *Hati* for the second time in four long months. When the door sealed, water began to flood in from the sides as the room filled slowly. Connor had a lot of time to think things over while he waited.

In his mind he imagined he was back in Healdsburg with his family. When he was four, he and Alex had gone into the woods to fight an imaginary battle with mythical creatures. They carried sticks like swords and spears and Alex would narrate the events happening around them. It always started small and would escalate into a grand adventure. On the particular day he was thinking about, Alex had mentioned a patrol of goblins sneaking through the forest toward the castle.

They snuck up together around the trees until Alex pointed to a small stump.

"There is the goblin scout. Get him, Connor!" Alex said eagerly.

Connor dashed out of the bushes, swinging his stick hard into the stump several times. Alex came up behind him frantically.

"It's a trap! Back to back!" Alex yelled.

They immediately stood back to back, fighting off the imaginary forces of the goblin patrol. Alex took an arrow to the knee and cried out as he fell to the ground. Connor stepped over him, swinging his sword mightily. He could still imagine how the goblins looked to him as he fought them away until they were all dead.

Alex would get up and pretend to bandage his knee while Connor would move to the edge of the clearing looking ahead at what Alex described as, "the lair of the giant." The giant, in their game, always ended up being William, who would always stop whatever he was doing to play with them. He was fun like that.

They crept through the woods until they came to the edge of their yard, climbing up a tree and out on a branch that took them over the fence into the backyard. They climbed down a rope they had tied on that branch years before and onto the grass.

"Once we cross the river, we'll be in the lair of the giant. Be careful," Alex said quietly.

Connor nodded and the two boys crawled on their bellies toward the lap-lane portion of their pool, which was next to the oriental-style gym. As they got closer they could hear the grunting of the giant inside. The boys moved into the water and came out on the other side, soaking wet. Around to the back entrance, they crawled until they could see the giant's form.

The man was pounding away at a punching bag, lathered in sweat. He seemed intent on the bag as he laid into it with heavy hits and quick kicks. He'd been at it for nearly thirty minutes, so the boys knew he must be tired.

With a yell, Connor and Alex charged into the lair of the giant, swords held high. William immediately turned and fought off the furious assault, quickly disarming the boys with a growl.

"What am I today then?" he asked with a big smile on his face as he threw Connor over his shoulder.

"A terrible giant!" Connor screamed as William started to tickle him.

"Rah!" William growled, grabbing out at Alex with his free hand while Connor squirmed away to get free.

The three boys played for several minutes, William chasing the boys around the yard playfully. When they got tired, Connor collapsed to the ground, turning over at the last second before the giant got him to plunge a make-believe knife into the monster's eyes.

There in the grass, the giant lay dead. The children celebrated by going to the refrigerator that was near the outdoor kitchen and grabbing sodas. Afterwards, they all swam in the pool together. Connor even remembered seeing his mom reading by the pool, watching their game with a smile on her face. That was the last memory Connor had before his mom died.

The water had been full in the dome for nearly three minutes when Connor finally started paying attention again. He had been enjoying the memory with such clarity he had completed tuned out the rest of the world. He was surprised to find that he wasn't crying at the memory of his mother and stepfather, since normally thinking about them made him sad.

He felt somehow invigorated though, glad to be able to still remember that sort of thing. Shaking off the nostalgia, Connor activated his propulsion systems and felt *Hati* lift off the ground, through the water and out into the ocean.

"There you are, kid, thought you drowned or something," Vertigo said over the communicator.

"No, I was just thinking." Connor figured that Vertigo had been tracking him on his motion sensor.

"Well, get your head in the game, we have to meet up with the Battle Frigates at Station Sigma on Mars."

"How long is that going to take?"

"It takes normal ships about a week. But we're going to slipstream."

Connor was just starting to see sunlight as he came up through the water. When he burst from the waves, he came face to face with the *Fenris*.

"Wow, that Battle Suit is huge!" Connor said excitedly.

"Yeah, the UEDF modeled it after your ship, but added some extra armor and firepower," Vertigo explained.

Not wanting to be outdone, Connor added, "It looks slow."

"Yeah, it kind of is," Vertigo admitted. "Are you ready yet?"

"Sure, let's go."

The two ships flew high up into the sky, through the clouds and out into space. Connor opened the slipstream consciously between Earth and Mars, and the two vessels proceeded through.

—

From the time they left Aeris VII until the time they reached the Sol system was seventeen days, four hours, twelve minutes, and fifty-two seconds. To Alex and Marlena, it felt like only a couple of minutes had passed. They emerged well ahead of the battle group that had fled Aeris nearly a month before. They weren't sure of the time, but if the frigates had an average jump, Alex and Marlena could be waiting for weeks.

They had known that it would probably be a while before the frigates caught up to *Skoll's* remarkable slipstream abilities, but they also knew that they had to be prepared just in case the group got lucky with their jump.

"Do you ever get the feeling that Balvoon was lying to us?" Alex asked, while sitting in the gunner's chair of the flight deck.

"I don't think so. I think I would have been able to tell," Marlena replied confidently.

"I just have to wonder if an invasion would really hinge on the success of one small attack."

"I understand; I had that same thought. But they did have intelligence that our forces were spread thin, so they thought they could establish a foothold. With the way slipstream drives go, you never know if your intelligence is accurate at eight thousand light years."

"So if they have someone spying on us, why didn't the spy just report the success of an attack, rather than wait for a column of frigates?"

"Maybe Harruhama feared we would intercept his spy and send him false data?" Marlena suggested, not really sure what the answer was.

It sounded plausible enough for Alex. He knew that reliable data transfer would be difficult with spies that far out into the colonies.

"Mom, I've been wondering for a long time, but never been able to figure something out," Alex began, changing the subject while the two looked out the small windows at the endless night beyond.

"What's that?"

"Why don't the people of Earth develop other resources, rather than trying to enslave the colonies?"

"That's a good question, Alex. I think William would have been better at explaining an answer like that, he was far better with political motives than I am."

"It just seems like there would be enough stuff in the galaxy that we could trade it, you know? I don't understand why a military leader would want to rule people."

Marlena smiled at her son. He was intelligent for his age

and asking all the right kind of questions. She knew that he was going to make an excellent leader someday.

A red sensor alert interrupted the conversation.

"Looks like we're not alone out here," Marlena said suddenly.

"Should I slipstream us away?" Alex asked hesitantly.

"No, let's see who it is. We can always slipstream if there's a problem."

The two watched on the sensors as a large group of ships moved in their direction. At this sensor range, it would take hours before they could even identify the vessels, let alone hail them, so they sat back to wait. They didn't wait as long as they thought they would watching as the blips on the sensor jumped, closing half the distance.

"Someone is slipstreaming them toward us," Marlena said, sitting upright in her chair.

The blips closed the distance farther, bringing them into a higher sensor detail range.

Alex moved over to the navigation station to watch the reports come in from the computer.

"Looks like two small vessels and five Battle Frigates," Alex announced.

"Looks like a bad attempt at an ambush," Marlena agreed.

"I know, right? Insulting that they think they have a chance against us," Alex said with a laugh. "Should I sound the retreat?"

Marlena laughed despite herself. She knew better than to underestimate Harruhama this close to Earth. From what she could tell, they were in Mars' orbit but on the opposite side of Sol from the red planet.

"No, but why don't you go suit up, before they slipstream right on top of us. Be careful out there. We're not taking any chances, Alex," Marlena warned, giving her son a quick hug.

"I'll be fine, Mom," Alex said, smiling as he went down the stairs into the crew quarters and onto the cargo bay.

—

The battle group was progressing smoothly using a series of small slipstreams to close the gap between them and the Gortha ship.

Connor was getting pretty good at streaming to exactly where he wanted as he bounced his way over to his enemy. The ship had appeared on his sensor a long time before it had been reported by Vertigo. Connor decided to keep the information to himself, since he wasn't sure why they were waiting to say anything.

He was confused that his instruments, which were so accurate at reporting location and distance, even ahead of the *Fenris*, were having trouble giving him any details about his enemies. To his flight computer, he was looking at a generic Gortha attack ship.

"I expected something worse," Connor said to himself.

"Worse than you think," a voice replied in a whisper.

"What is that supposed to mean?" he asked, but got no reply.

Connor was getting a bad feeling in the pit of his stomach as he got into visual range of the vessel. He felt like he was supposed to remember something, like something in a dream. But he couldn't quite place it. The thought was lost to him when he looked out at the ship and felt a wave of nausea overtake him.

"I am unable to verify the Gortha ship. My instruments are giving me some kind of feedback," Connor said into his communicator.

"I have experienced that before; their ships do that. You have to focus through it and relax. Use your instruments and fight hard," Vertigo's voice sounded over the headset as a reply.

Something didn't sit right with Connor. In none of their simulations did the Gortha ships behave that way.

"A second ship has emerged from the first, everyone be ready to fire," Vertigo said.

"Wait, when did you fight Gortha before?" Connor asked, the pieces of the puzzle not fitting together in his head.

"Eagle Nebula; don't worry about it, it's time to focus, kid."

Connor thought hard through the waves of confusion. He'd known Austin was aboard the *Griswold* when he saved it and had known that battle wasn't against Gortha, but against some kind of a rebel faction. Adam Malavich from Atmos XI had told him that it wasn't a Gortha attack.

"All ships, engage!" the order sounded over the communicator.

Connor watched as a Ra squadron flew forward at the second Gortha ship, which had emerged from the first. The larger Battle Frigates began firing auto cannons at the two ships, which separated quickly. They moved fast and with the most precise flying Connor had ever witnessed. Before *Hati* or *Fenris* had even moved, five of the RA fighters were down.

—

"Mom, that's the ship that Jordon Malavich described!" Alex screamed into his communicator while he was flying circles around the incoming cannon fire. All the ships and weapons seemed slow to him; he felt like he could take down an entire fleet in *Skoll*.

"Which ship?" Marlena's voice was calm, like she was talking a walk.

"The wolf-faced armor with seven wings! Mom, I think that's Connor!" Alex said, his voice rising with the gravity of fighting his brother.

As he spoke the two opposing Battle Suit Vessels began to attack. The larger one moved toward the *Tizona* and the smaller, toward *Skoll*.

"Mom, be careful of that thing. It looks slow, but I know what these suits can do," Alex warned as he disabled another Ra fighter.

A voice crackled in Alex's head as he turned to face the black suit coming in at him. "Hati!" it exclaimed like it was greeting an old friend, or family member.

Alex shook the thought away, and focused on raising his defenses. Fully armored, he danced *Skoll* back as the ship *Hati* came in with a furious charge. Alex knew it was his brother piloting the ship before he saw the boy's face in the cockpit. It moved with precision and skill that no other pilot would have had a chance to match. Alex backed away, desperately trying to open a communication line to his brother while fending off the barrage of attacks coming from the ship.

Marlena had no trouble staying ahead of the larger Battle Suit, but was beginning to feel the stress of Ra fighters trying to flank her and heavy cannon fire from the larger Battle Frigates. She had no time to focus on what her sons might be doing, instead relying on instinct to stay alive. She was gaining ground in the battle, taking down two Ra fighters in a spinning maneuver while she fired her own cannons, then the larger battle suit launched a barrage of missiles her way.

—

He was confused and frustrated. Connor found that if he looked directly at the Gortha ship, he felt sick to his stomach. He was throwing everything he had at it, with the support of five Frigates and the remains of a squadron of Ra fighters, to no avail. The ship was too fast and managed to avoid his attacks like it knew they were coming. To make matters worse, the whispers in his head seemed to be weeping and saying the word "Skoll" over and over again.

Then the voice over the communicator changed. For an instant, it sounded like it was going to say his name, "Con." It sounded surprised, but ended with a squealing garble of strange Gortha words. The strange language made Connor even more nauseated and he began having to focus on his breathing rather than the fight.

The ship he was after was making short work of the Ra fighters, but had not attacked him at all. No matter how hard Connor came on, the ship would just dance away, leaving him unharmed. The pieces of the puzzle were coming together slowly in his head. Until it hit him that Alex had turned against the UEDF and in a fight that Vertigo had claimed was Gortha.

The Gortha ship grabbed *Hati* by the shoulders and spun around to the back side, putting itself against his back and fighting off the last of the Ra fighters from there.

"Back to back," Connor said to himself, tears filling his chocolate-colored eyes.

"Back to back," the voice in his head confirmed.

"Alex?" Connor said into the com.

—

From his position in the Battle Frigate *Nostus*, Flagship of the 1st fleet, General Harruhama watched the battle with a feeling of growing anxiety. He had been monitoring the communications, and had watched his Ra squadrons get destroyed by the two legendary ships, *Tizona* and *Skoll*. When *Hati* and *Fenris* joined the fight, he'd thought the tide would turn, and was frustrated when the two other ships managed to hold their ground.

The operative on Aeris VII had given him good intelligence

on when the two ships, which were proving to be a huge thorn in his side, would be attempting to arrive in the Sol system ahead of the convoy retreating from the battle in the Hourglass Nebula. Harruhama had figured that with his two prized Battle Suit Vessels and a standard Battle Group he could overwhelm two small ships. He was beginning to feel that he might be wrong.

Vertigo and Raptor had been reporting back the confusion brought on by their 4th inhibitor chips working properly, but had continued to attack, until now. Harruhama was watching *Skoll* take position at the back of *Hati*, and heard Connor's voice over the com.

"Alex?" the voice asked.

"What are you talking about, Raptor?" came Vertigo's reply.

It was getting out of hand very quickly.

"I think this Gortha ship is my brother! I think we're being tricked!" Raptor exclaimed as he turned his ship to attack the Battle Frigates.

"Don't believe it, kid! The Gortha are tricking you, like they tricked your brother!" Vertigo said quickly.

"You're an idiot," Connor retorted as *Hati* began firing upon one of the Frigates.

General Harruhama had heard enough. He knew it was a gamble to bring the boy out here, but he'd hoped it would pay off. It did not.

From the commander station on the Nostus, General Harruhama reluctantly began entering the codes for the "Inhibitor Contingency."

～

Deep in the virtual world of his OMBI, the subconscious apparition of Connor Pereira was working on developing a new attack plan for a space battle, with a box of crayons and a piece of white paper. He was sitting on a grassy hill under a tree with his friends Omega and Hati, who was in a wolfish form.

They had been laughing a moment ago, until the world had grown dark.

"What's happening?" Connor asked.

"They are trying to kill us," Omega replied.

"Why?" Connor asked, his voice filled with trepidation.

"That doesn't matter. The blocks that were installed are being overloaded. We don't have much time," Omega said, looking at Hati.

The wolf whimpered softly and dissipated from the virtual world. Omega looked at Connor, putting his hand on the boy's shoulder.

"I am sorry, my friend, this is where we say goodbye," Omega said with a smile.

"Am I going to die?" Connor asked quietly.

"I hope not. I am routing out the sync connects we have made."

"I don't understand!" Connor cried desperately.

As if in response, a large bomb appeared on the ground beside them, the countdown timer moving downward quickly.

Omega put his hand on Connor's shoulder and smiled.

"You have been a good friend, Connor," he said as he began to shield Connor from the bomb as best he could.

—

In the cockpit of *Hati*, Connor's conscious mind felt the change. The ship had disconnected itself from his consciousness and began to drift slightly. Worse, his OMBI had started growing hot on his arm and he felt a profound sense of sadness.

He glanced outside of his window to see his brother's face looking back at him and smiling. Then he felt his arm erupt in pain. As the inhibitors detonated, the connection between the boy and the OMBI ceased, causing ripples of agony to shoot through his body.

It wasn't quick; the shock caused Connor to go into convulsions. He could feel the blood pouring from his nose as his body slammed around the cockpit. All his muscles tensed at once, and the air was forced out of his lungs, leaving him struggling for breath. He forced his eyes open to see the control panel rushing up to meet him, and then, nothing.

Alex watched his brother collapse with a feeling of helpless desperation. As a wave of anger washed over him, he turned the full force of his weapons upon the Frigates, meaning to destroy them all without mercy. As he began to fire, he felt something heavy hit him in the side.

The large Battle Suit Vessel tackled him hard, knocking him away from where his brother's ship lifelessly drifted. Alex took a quick look at his sensor and saw *Tizona* coming back from its desperate maneuver between the Battle Frigates to dodge the barrage of missiles the other ship had fired.

As he faced off with the other Battle Suit, he could see the familiar face of Austin Hughes in the cockpit and shook his head. The two clashed, as they had many times, twin swords bouncing hard against a longer blade and shield. Alex knew he had to focus to win this fight and could not spare any distraction. All the same, he opened a communication channel.

"Mom, Connor is down. I think they detonated his OMBI," Alex said briefly into the mic.

He heard her screaming on the other side, trying to deny the fact that her youngest son could be dead. Alex advanced forward quickly, putting Vertigo on the defensive, sweeping his swords back and forth to buy himself some time.

"He could still be alive, Mom; we have to get him out of here, now," Alex said, trying to remain calm and focused.

Vertigo pushed him back with several heavy swings from the larger ship. Alex could feel the strength behind the swings as he attempted to deflect them and realized he was going to have to outthink his old friend quickly, until Marlena stepped in.

Tizona hit the larger Battle Suit Vessel on its side with a barrage of heavy cannon fire that sent it spinning sideways for a brief moment. Free from the fight temporarily and still dodging the heavy Cannons of the Battle Frigates, *Skoll* grabbed the side of *Tizona* and held on until they were next to where *Hati* was floating inert thorough the battlefield.

"Put him in the cargo hold. Let's get out of here, Alex!" Marlena ordered over the com.

Alex grabbed *Hati* with *Skoll's* powerful hands and pushed the ship into the open cargo hold with all his might. When he was secured, Alex began the process of opening a slipstream portal back to Aeris VII.

"Hold on, Mom, almost got it!" Alex said quickly, focusing on the portal.

"Alex, he's secure, let's..." Marlena began, but ended suddenly.

The portal opened ahead of the ships and Alex began guiding *Tizona* through.

"Mom, what's wrong? Mom!?" Alex was screaming into his communicator when he got hit from the side.

—

She had seen the man out of the corner of her eye before he charged. She managed to get out of her seat and roll to the side, avoiding the knife blade entirely. The plain-looking man grinned at her as he advanced with the knife, Marlena running out of room quickly.

She felt the ship lurch suddenly, and, using the distraction, came forward quickly landing a few light punches before rolling behind the assassin and running down the steps into the crew quarters. Looking back up past the man, she could see the fading image of *Skoll* fighting off the larger Battle Suit Vessel as *Tizona* moved through the slipstream.

The man moved slowly down the stairs toward her, measuring her ability with his eyes. The operative walked with the poise of a cat hunting its prey.

"Nicely done, most don't see it coming."

Marlena didn't reply as she picked herself up off the floor. Her mind was somewhere between the plight of her two sons and the man preventing her from saving them. She was unarmed, but had weapons stashed all over the ship. She took a step back toward the cargo hold, causing the man to come on quickly.

He slashed forward with his knife, just missing her neck before reversing the direction of the blade and coming down hard at her chest. To her credit, Marlena moved with the grace of a seasoned warrior, staying a step ahead of the deadly dagger. The man had tried to finish it quick; he knew better than to underestimate this woman who was his primary target, the leader of the Independent Colonies, the war hero, the mother of the only person to ever fight him to a standstill.

She had the appearance of a girl, but the spirit of a lion, and the operative was not going to fail a second time. She managed to stay ahead of his weapon, backing off into the cargo hold where the large, white wolf-knight suit lay crumpled on the floor. As he came on, the woman fell back over the railing of the walkway, onto the top of a crate, and ran over to a storage locker. The assassin followed as quickly as he could, trying to prevent the woman from getting access to a weapon.

As it was, he was almost too late, the handgun rising in time to fire off a shot before his dagger plunged into the woman's side.

The two held their pose for a moment until the man staggered backwards. He could feel that the bullet bruised him beneath his armor but came on with his dagger again.

Marlena screamed with rage as she unloaded the gun into the man's chest and face, pulling the trigger long after the weapon had ran out of ammo.

She was breathing heavily as blood soaked her flight suit on the right side of her body. In the same locker, she grabbed a medical kit and gave herself a shot of local anesthetic for the pain before patching the wound with a synthetic binding gel. She knew that it was by no means taken care of, but for the moment the wound wouldn't kill her.

Grabbing a crowbar off the wall, she walked slowly over to where *Hati* lay face down on the floor of her cargo bay and, in pain, climbed to the back and pried at the cockpit. Fortunately as she began, the armor opened up, seemingly on its own. Inside she saw the crumpled form of her youngest son.

With all her strength she pulled the boy out of his ship and carried him up the stairs into the crew quarters. She placed him gently upon her bed and began to evaluate his wounds. He didn't appear to suffer from any physical damage, other than the blood that was drying under his nose and a few bruises. His OMBI was smoldering and, despite her best effort, wouldn't come off the boy's arm.

She leaned close to his chest and sighed heavily when she heard him breathing. Tears flowed from her almond-colored eyes as she passed out from her wound next to her baby boy.

CHAPTER 19

Against the current

S EEING HIS MOTHER AND BROTHER MAKE IT THROUGH
the slipstream, Alex turned his attention back on the fight.
He didn't like the odds too much, with five Battle Frigates
firing on him and a large Battle Suit Vessel hammering down on
him. It took some effort, but he managed to focus on the task
ahead, calming his anxiety with a deep breath.

The fight got worse for him as two more Ra squadrons
launched from the frigates and Alex found himself fighting defensively to avoid taking damage. The pressure from Vertigo was
intense; he'd clearly been training for this specific fight and his
form was nearly perfect. Alex knew he could outsmart him eventually, but he was spending too much of his effort reacting to the
fluctuating battle to be able to think for even a moment.

He felt himself getting tired after more than an hour of
fighting, and knew he was going to have to do something soon
or risk getting destroyed.

Fenris came in hard, swinging its long sword in a downward arc that Alex caught with his left blade. Using the blade in
his right hand, Alex slammed the armored hull of the larger ship
several times. The effort cost him several hits from Ra Fighter
cannons against his force field.

He was getting frustrated that they were able to whittle

down his defenses like this. The increasing amount of concentration to keep his armor and shields up was causing him to sweat and feel dizzy. He knew he wouldn't get a chance to slipstream without at least a few moments' reprieve, and certainly not enough for the long jump back to Aeris.

His mind was whirling with half-made plans and ideas, trying to get a break for even a moment to get his bearings. *Fenris* slammed into him again and he felt his external armor dissipate from the blow. He knew it was about to be over as the larger vessel grappled him with heavy arms and began to squeeze.

Alex forced his mind to relax as he focused on escape. Not sure why he chose it, Alex thought about his bedroom in the house he grew up in and how safe it felt knowing that his family was close by. The stars around him rippled as he felt himself fall through the slipstream.

On the other side, with *Fenris* still clinging tightly to *Skoll*, Alex found himself in Earth's orbit. He realized his mistake almost immediately as the planetary defense platforms began to rotate and fire at him. He tried to turn so that Vertigo would absorb the brunt of the heavy cannon fire. It didn't go perfectly, but after a couple of hits he managed to get his adversary to release him. Vertigo flew back and watched as the cannons overwhelmed the smaller vessel.

Alex felt the impacts against his hull as if they were fists pounding into his body. *Skoll's* hard, strange metal body did a good job absorbing most of the impact. But he could feel the vessel weakening under the barrage.

He turned his thrusters downward and fired them as hard as he could, plunging through the atmosphere of Earth down toward the planet below. The ship began to heat up quickly as Alex tried to level his descent. The damage he had taken prevented him from maneuvering too well, but he managed to avoid being cooked alive in the cockpit of *Skoll*.

It seemed like he was falling for a long time, and looking downward he saw the familiar coastline of California as he aimed himself toward the bay. He fired his reverse thrusters as he neared the water and managed to slow himself as *Skoll* splashed down near Golden Gate Bridge.

The ship sunk down and came to a rest at the bottom in the shallow water. Alex took a deep breath and rested a moment, accessing *Skoll* through his OMBI. He could feel the ship making repairs to itself, using the minerals of the water and sand around it. Alex wasn't sure he believed that it was possible, but his OMBI's connection to his ship gave him the distinct feeling that it would be ready for battle again.

He wasn't sure how long it would take, but he somehow knew it would take longer than he could afford to wait in the cockpit without food or water. He took a deep breath and opened the rear hatch, feeling the cold water of the San Francisco Bay rush in to meet him. When the cockpit was full, he emerged into the water and swam upwards toward daylight.

He came out of the water only a few hundred feet from shore and swam to the abandoned coastline to find that the city had been left in ruins. Buildings crumbled all around and the streets were blasted apart from the fighting. Apparently the riots on Earth had become an all-out revolution.

Alex took a deep breath and shut his eyes. He calmed himself down by breathing deep and started making himself a mental to-do list: food, water and shelter. A new goal in mind, Alex walked on unsteady legs into the city.

—

William had been fighting back waves of UEDF soldiers for the last three days in Seattle, Washington when he received a hand-written note from a messenger. The kid he put in charge of monitoring enemy communications in the warehouse near the pier that they'd been using as a base had sent him the message.

'Strange enemy chatter from California; High Value Target in play' the message read in scribbled handwriting.

William Mercer didn't know who it could be that the enemy forces were trying to eliminate, but he thought that if it was important to Harruhama, it should be important to him. The battle lines had be set on the streets in the city and no one was moving for the time being, so he walked back with the boy who had delivered the message all the way down to the pier.

Most of the buildings in Seattle had taken damage; only a few seemed unmolested by the war in the streets. As he walked through the blasted streets of Emerald City, William began to wonder if the cost of the revolution had been worth the goals. It had escalated beyond his original message of deception and murder when the guards in New York began firing upon the crowd. When the true colors of the EMC emerged, the people rose up.

Walking into the warehouse, the man was nearly overwhelmed by the activity of the citizens, now fully organized against the EMC, taking messages and orders around to field commanders. The place seemed to hum with energy and, as he walked in, the people turned to cheer his name. "Dragoon," they called him, celebrating the man who led them.

William accepted that he was not as much a leader of the revolution as a figurehead, but he knew that the people needed icons to rally around. The men who had assumed command of the various rebel factions had warned him to stay alive at all costs. Even so, he had always found himself on the front lines, fighting beside the soldiers who were laying down their lives for the cause. He fought beside them every day, trying to throw out the oppressive regime of General Harruhama and the EMC.

When he got to the communication station, he asked for clarification on the note he had received.

"Sir, the enemy leaders are moving in all available soldiers to seek out and destroy a target they are referring to as "Driftwood." Apparently they want him bad enough that battalions are leaving the front lines to find out where he went."

"Where is he at?" William asked the boy.

"From what I can tell, he crash landed in San Francisco seventeen minutes ago."

"Crash landed? Then he is either from the colonies or a defector. Either way, if they want him so bad, we should pull him out of there."

"Yes, sir, we don't have many organized units in that area, but I will rally whoever we can to fortify the crash site."

"I'm going down there too," William stated calmly.

He wasn't sure why he felt that it was so important to leave Seattle and go back to San Francisco, but somewhere in his gut, he felt like it was the place he should be.

Ten minutes later he was aboard the VS91-transport he had flown in on, flying high above the city and heading south. Still piloting the ship, Jared Blackwell told him it would take a couple of hours, but William told him to hurry all the same.

—

As it turned out, Alex didn't have to walk very far to find shelter. He came up into the Presidio of San Francisco into the Old Coast Guard Station, where he found a small outpost. As he got closer, the men standing guard pointed weapons his way and yelled at him to approach with his hands raised.

Alex did as he was instructed, as these were not soldiers, but civilians. When he got close enough he yelled out to them.

"I am with the 'Independent Colonies' against the UEDF, we are on the side of the 'Free Men'!" he yelled.

The men seemed to ease up and yelled for him to get closer. When he got to the doors, they let him inside. The inside of the guard station had been transformed into a temporary barracks for these men, who offered him food and water.

Alex drank and ate while telling them where he had come from. They didn't seem to have a leader, telling Alex that the man who had brought them to this place had been shot a few days before by UEDF soldiers. Naturally the boy volunteered for the job.

"We need to set up a perimeter and make sure we aren't cornered here. How many men do we have?"

"Eighteen," one man informed.

"Okay then, nineteen now. What are your names?"

The men spoke quietly, obviously tired from the fighting. Getting all their names, Alex introduced himself and they set about fortifying the old building.

After a few minutes, commotion broke out on the lawn outside the station as another unit of nearly sixty Free Men arrived. Stating that they had orders to come looking for a UEDF target, they were welcomed by the men at the outpost. When they saw Alex, they seemed relieved and informed him that they had been ordered by their commanders up north to protect him. Those same soldiers sent reports back to their commanders as scouts went out to rally other bands of Free Men until after a couple of hours; Alex had a small army of almost a thousand soldiers at his command.

The Free Men quickly filled the old barracks and aircraft hangers of the Presidio, awaiting their orders. Bad news came with the last group of revolutionaries when they informed him that a massive force of UEDF soldiers was also approaching their location looking for Alex, with them a large Battle Suit Vessel.

～

Knowing he was outnumbered and probably didn't have a weapon available that could damage *Fenris*, Alex set his troops into fortified, defensive positions in the hills, around trees and in buildings. He didn't have much of a plan to fight a better-armed force, except to use the terrain to his advantage as much as possible. He knew that Vertigo was with the enemy force and would see that he committed most of his defenses around old Fort Winfield Scott's officers housing, deep in the Presidio. He hoped the ruse would give him the surprise he needed.

Once his troops were deployed, Alex climbed the long of-framp up to where Highway 101 became the Presidio Parkway. High above his chosen battlefield, he watched a large enemy force move in from the East, led by *Fenris* and a smaller force enter from the South. The large Battle Armor Vessel walked slowly, scanning the area. Alex held very still, knowing that Austin favored his motion sensor to visual cues and hoped that his friend's habits hadn't changed in the past four months. As it was, the wind had died down and the grounds were still. No doubt some of the soldiers laying in ambush were moving, but Austin wouldn't be worried about any kind of a weapon that the ground force would have.

As they moved through the Main Post of the Presidio, the two enemy forces connected and began proceeding west toward the old officer's housing. When they crossed under the bridge Alex was waiting on, he pushed against an abandoned car that was hanging precariously from the edge of the bridge. His strength enhanced by his OMBI, Alex managed to budge the car without too much effort. The vehicle fell down almost right on top of *Fenris* before it detonated from the dynamite that Alex had manifested into it though his neuro-sync. The blast knocked *Fenris* back, along with engulfing a large number of UEDF soldiers in flames.

The Free Men soldiers began to pop out from their hiding places, spraying small arms and machine-gun fire into the surprised soldiers. The ambush started off successfully as, no doubt the UEDF troops had not been expecting Alex to have rallied so many defenders.

Alex manifested a four-tubed rocket launcher from his OMBI, being one of the strongest weapons he had available, and fired downward on the staggered Battle Suit as it attempted to gain its footing. The rockets knocked it onto the ground, but didn't do much real damage to the heavy vessel.

Unfortunately, Alex didn't have anything better to hit it with, so he kept the barrage going as quickly as he could manifest new rockets. He noticed that Austin hadn't raised his armor or force field, recognizing that the natural hull of *Fenris* was enough to defeat anything that Alex, on foot, could hit it with.

Alex reached through his OMBI out toward *Skoll* and tried to determine if the ship was ready for another battle, but it occurred to him that it might be a lot longer than he hoped. Focusing instead on the battle below, Alex fired another rocket barrage for good measure and ran down the street toward the city. He moved with the grace of a cat, his legs enhanced by his OMBI's connection to his body. As he ran on, the bridge exploded behind him and he felt himself flying forward.

Apparently Austin had enough of getting attacked from above, and decided to destroy the bridge. Huge pieces of rubble rained down below the bridge, causing chaos in the ranks of both armies. Alex raised his own armor before he slammed into the car in front of him. Even armored he felt the impact rattle through him as he bounced off the vehicle.

His strange metal armor made sparks against the ground as he skidded to a stop. He was just getting to his feet when *Fenris* leapt up onto the remains of the bridge and came toward him. Alex knew he was in trouble; he couldn't defeat Austin head to head while the other boy had such an advantage. The armies below were slaughtering each other by the score, the Free Men using their defensive position to inflict massive damage on the UEDF troops.

Alex raised his force field in time to absorb the impact of a stream of large chain gun fire from *Fenris*, which brought the shield right back down again. He knew Austin was toying with him now and that he didn't have anywhere to run.

Behind the Battle Suit, a VS91-transport shuttle appeared on the horizon, coming in very quickly. Alex had thought his enemy was about to get reinforcements until he noticed the thing setting a collision course with the battle armor that was bearing down on him.

Alex reached through his OMBI, focusing on *Fenris*, which was under the complete control of Vertigo. He felt the machine's body physically changing as Austin manifested a long sword. He reached farther inside, finding the CPU and grabbing at it with all his force of will. He was not the pilot of the ship, so he was at a severe disadvantage in taking control away from Austin. Alex had never tried to disrupt someone else's vehicle before but found that he was able to at least stop it from advancing for a short time.

He felt like he was in a battle of wills with his old friend, a fight where the other boy had every advantage. Alex tried everything he could to interrupt the sync between man and machine, but found himself thrown back out before too long.

"That was a nice try, Gortha pig!" the mechanical voice of Austin Hughes said through the speaker.

Fenris dropped the heavy sword, causing it to dissipate quickly, and instead manifested cannons on its arm, taking aim at

Alex's position on the bridge. Alex watched as the VS91-transport came in at full speed into *Fenris'* back, causing the large ship to lurch forward over the edge of the bridge and fall hard onto the ground below. Using the distraction, Alex reached through his OMBI again, grabbing out with his will at the larger machine, which was now more disconnected with its pilot. Unsure of exactly how he did it, Alex put it into a full shutdown cycle and locked the access with a random encryption as quickly as he could think of it.

He turned his attention to the transport, which had bounced off the Battle Suit and crashed at the edge of the Presidio into a line of houses. Alex ran as hard as he could to the crash site. Even with his enhanced speed, it took him several minutes before he got to the shuttle. He tried to open the door, but it was stuck. Reaching through his OMBI, Alex found a deep inner strength and ripped the door up, removing it from its track completely.

Climbing inside, Alex saw the dead pilot, crushed between the building and his seat. Further in, Alex saw the form of a man laying still, and barely breathing.

The man looked back at Alex and tears began to fill his dark-blue eyes. Alex moved quickly, grabbing a first aid kit off the wall and binding the man's bleeding leg as fast as he could.

"You..." the man tried to say.

"Shh, don't talk. I need to get you patched up and out of here before those soldiers arrive," Alex said quickly, focusing on the wound, which was bleeding badly.

The man reached up with an unsteady hand and pulled down the bandana that was covering his face, taking a deep breath.

Alex turned to see the face of William Mercer for the first time in six years.

"William! Oh my God! I'm going to get you out of here!" Alex's voice was on the edge of panic as he stuffed the injured leg with synthetic bonding gel.

"Alex…"

"What is it?" Alex asked, looking the man in his eyes.

"I'm proud of you, son," William managed to say, coughing between his words.

Smoke began to fill the transport and Alex knew he would have to risk moving his stepfather if they were going to have any hope of survival. Alex reached through his OMBI and felt around the area for anything that might help him. He could feel an AFMR somewhere to the north of him not too far away.

"I know you are, William. I need you to try to walk."

The man shook his head from side to side, coughing again as blood spurted from his mouth onto Alex's uniform. William grabbed Alex firmly by the arm.

"Your mother … would be proud of … you too," William said, struggling to keep his eyes open.

Alex gripped the man's hand as tightly as he could, looking him right in the eye.

"She is proud of me, William," Alex said quietly. "Mom is alive."

CHAPTER 20

Undaunted

TWO HUNDRED AND THIRTY-NINE FEET OFF THE COAST of Breaker Beach, San Francisco, the Battle Armor Vessel called *Skoll* was quietly absorbing the minerals from the water and sand. The deconstruction of the elements took time, but slowly the ship had enough raw elemental data to reconstruct useful materials. It began with the vital systems, slowly removing the damaged parts, replacing them with new ones. The damaged pieces were deconstructed and reformed into new pieces, which fit over different areas of the ship.

So it went on for hours and days, piece by piece repairing the damage it had taken, trying to be made whole again. Inside the CPU, the virtual intelligence could sense that its operator was in danger, but could do nothing to help him. *Skoll* cried out, but received no reply.

—

Two miles from where he had crash landed, a sixteen-year-old boy with striking green eyes, enhanced by the power of an alien technology, carried the body of his stepfather to the north as quickly as he could. The sounds of battle continued behind him and he could see that several squads of soldiers broke off from the main group, to give chase to the target they had come to kill.

Covering nearly a mile inside six minutes, even with the weight of the man in his arms, Alex burst into the California Pacific Medical Center, frantically searching for a medical robot that could assist him. He pushed past patients and administrators, forcing his way deep into the interior of the hospital with soldiers coming in right behind him. The staff and patients screamed and fled, slowing the soldiers trying to get in. Alex found a room at the end of the hall, and, using the power of his OMBI, began summoning the 311 Anti-Fire and Medical Robots from all over the hospital.

They marched slowly, like an army of robot zombies, through the halls in the direction of the call. When the first one arrived, Alex ordered it to help the man in any way possible. The robot removed enough of the man's battle suit to see his wounds and began evaluating them with the thin green light projecting from its one eye.

"Prognosis: Deceased"

"No!" Alex screamed, denying the claim.

Alex used his OMBI to override the machine's protocol and ordered it to revive the man.

As more 311AFMR began to approach, Alex heard the sounds of soldiers in the hallways encircling his position. Closing his eyes and taking a deep breath, Alex manifested a mounted machine gun with a sensor turret. He had no idea he could do that until now, but he needed time and his OMBI had responded. He even manifested wheels for the turret and rolled it down the hall. The weapon rolled to a stop and began firing at the fortified positions of the soldiers who had come to retrieve him.

Alex found that he only needed to maintain awareness of the weapon to keep it active, which wasn't hard with all the noise it was creating. He created two more for good measure and set one at the door and the other down the hall in the opposite direction. Maintaining three was more of a challenge, but as he steadied himself with a few deep breaths, he found that he could manage it well enough.

He turned his attention back on the man and the robots who were working hard to repair him. One had William's leg propped up with two of its arms and was stitching a wound internally with tiny finger-like appendages protruding from its third arm. Another was examining and re-setting what looked like a broken ankle that hadn't been allowed to heal right. A third had the man pushed onto his side, while it used two of its arms to stitch a wound on his back that Alex hadn't even seen until now. A fourth AFMR was manually pumping man's heart with fingers which elongated into his chest while simultaneously infusing him with a blood regeneration enhancer from a nearby table.

Alex felt his turret go down before he heard the explosion in the hall. He let the thing dissipate as he rolled the one at the door way down to replace the first. The second one didn't last long as the soldiers threw another set of grenades into the hallway. Alex knew he was running out of time quickly.

"Come on!" he yelled at the AFMR, who continued to work impassively.

Hearing footsteps, Alex manifested a grenade into his hand and threw it down the hallway.

"Come on, William!" Alex yelled again, looking at the body of the man who had saved him, the man who had raised his brother, the man who had been like a father to him.

"Mom never quit! She lived on even when they tried to kill her! She is alive, damn you! She still loves you! Now wake up, William!" Alex screamed.

The man's eyes shot open as he gasped for breath. The AFMR continue to work on him as he looked around the room, unsure of where he was or what he was doing.

A smile formed on Alex's face as his final turret fired down the hall, suppressing the soldiers who had come for him.

"She's alive?" he heard William say, turning to see the man with tears in his eyes.

"Yes, and she is leading the colonies in a rebellion like you're leading the people here on Earth. You are the Dragoon, right?" Alex asked, turning back to the hallway.

"Yeah, that's right," William said, fighting to remain conscious.

The AFMR simultaneously stepped away from the man and moved to the corners of the rooms. He had been revived, but despite his best efforts, he lacked the strength to stand.

"Okay then. We're getting out of here, now," Alex said.

His eyes flashed with a green glow as he focused. Before him he manifested an A25-Combat Drone; its hulking form filled up the hallway outside the examination room. The machine turned and began to march in the direction of the enemy soldiers, firing rockets and machine guns in a steady stream of destruction. Alex turned to face William, eyes full of a soft green glow.

"Are you coming?" Alex asked, reaching a hand out to his stepfather.

William accepted the hand with a grin. His legs were weak, but his stepson was strong, and the two walked out of the medical center, behind the heavy steps of the powerful drone, into a city torn by war.

EPILOGUE

WITH THE MANHUNT FOR THE DANGEROUS PILOT of *Skoll* fully underway and *Tizona* gone through a slipstream, General Harruhama didn't waste any time ordering the attack on Aeris VII. Without *Hati* or *Skoll* to pull them through, the normal slipstream jump between Earth and the Hourglass Nebula would take between ten and eleven weeks. Even at their full strength of thirty-three Battle Frigates, the Independent Colonies could not withstand an assault from the full force of the UEDF.

Harruhama had one hundred and fourteen active Battle Frigates, twenty-one Anubis Squads, and one hundred and forty Ra Squadrons still available at his command, ready to be wielded like a mighty fist. With the dangerous Battle Armor Vessels out of play, it would be easy to end the rebellion in the colonies and restore order to the Earth.

"Open a channel to the Commanders of fleets two, six, seven and eight," Harruhama said to his communications officer aboard the UEDF Nostus.

"Channel open, sir."

"My friends, the hour has come to rid the heavens of the resisting factions of the so-called "independent colonies." Their defenses are down and their leaders are missing. It is time to take back what we lost and restore order to the galaxy! Go forth with all your might and reclaim our empire!"

With the orders away for the full-scale invasion, General

Harruhama sat back in his chair, thinking about the problems he still had on Earth. He knew he had a lot of work ahead of him and began to lay out plans for the systematic disposal of the Free Men.

"Sir, Mr. Wilhelm on the line for you."

"Clear the bridge!" Harruhama ordered.

The man's face turned white as the men and woman serving aboard the UEDF *Nostus* exited the room.

A young man's face appeared upon the screen of his datapad when Harruhama took the call.

"General, what is the status of your search for the rebel leaders, both planet side and in the colonies?" the boyish voice of Articus Wilhelm said on the line.

The boyish features were misleading, since this particular boy never seemed to age. Harruhama knew better than to stare.

"We are currently in the process of hunting down The Dragoon. We have his location and strike teams are searching the ruins of San Francisco for him now. As for the colony leaders, I am awaiting confirmation that Phoenix is dead and the assault on Aeris VII should take care of Velez, Gellar, Watson, and Clarke."

"Then you have nothing confirmed. They are still a threat," the boy chastised the General.

"Sir, with all due respect, plans are in motion. We are moving over one hundred Frigates toward the Hour Glass Nebula as we speak!" Harruhama pleaded.

"See that it is taken care of. We cannot suffer those dissidents any longer. You see what waiting has cost us? We have almost lost Earth!"

"I assure you that we are making every effort to correct the situation. You know that I am aware of how this works. I will do my part; please be patient."

"Either you will, General, or we will find someone else who can," Wilhelm warned.

The transmission ended, and General Harruhama was left to ponder the gravity of the threat.

—

Five thousand light years from Earth, in the Omega Nebula on the planet Dytopa II and approximately sixty-three miles from the city of Tiberius Falls, while searching the rocky coast of the Scorpio Sea, Doctor Miles Arminus and his partner Ethan Pereira found what they were looking for. The sensor equipment in their all-terrain vehicle picked up a strange metal composite a few weeks before, but due to the advent of a large monster storm he had put off his expedition.

Now, together on the shoreline, the two men had begun searching for the object that was giving off the strange readings. As they approached a small outcropping along the rocks, they saw something glittering off the bright white light of the White Dwarf star that Dytopa orbited.

The silver glint caught Dr. Arminus' eye and he proceeded toward the area. As he cleared the rubble away with a sonic pick, he saw a large silver door ahead of him. However, even with the pick he couldn't get the door open. Looking back at the log on his datapad, he realized that this was the entrance to a massive structure buried deep into the cliff face.

The howl of some nearby beast startled the man.

"Doctor Arminus, we need to head in or back to the truck, soon," Ethan said urgently, his eyes scanning the treeline.

He removed his large battle rifle from his shoulder slowly. Ethan was better than Arminus' previous pathfinder, who had failed to detect a mist wolf in their first expedition. Ethan's eyes never missed anything.

A shriek sounded from the opposite side, causing Arminus to jump. Ethan didn't flinch.

"We need to go, they are surrounding us," Ethan cautioned.

Packing up their gear quickly, they returned to their vehicle and began the long drive back to Tiberius Falls to report the discovery to the Independent Council of Colonies.

—

She awoke to the rhythm of a soft snoring sound. Marlena sat up against the pain of the wound in her side, the motion activating the lights in the crew quarters of her ship. Looking down, she saw her youngest son asleep, snoring softly. She smiled despite her pain at the serene look upon his face. His body seemed completely fine, but when she tried to wake him, she found that she could not.

Her smile gone, Marlena examined the device on her son's arm. It was well-worn and clearly damaged from the explosion of the inhibitor chip inside. She took a deep breath and slowly got up, turning around at the door to look at her son again. She had missed her baby boy and he had grown so much over the past six years she could hardly believe it.

She turned to look at the picture of her husband on the wall, the smiling face of William Mercer. She kissed her fingertips and pressed her hand to the picture with a tear in her eye.

"Thank you for taking such good care of him, baby," she said to the photo of the man she thought was dead.

With heavy steps, she walked up the stairs to the flight deck of the *Tizona*. Sitting heavily in her chair, she began a sensor sweep of the area to find out where she had gone in the slipstream. She was relieved to find that she was not far from Aeris VII. Alex had put her within a couple of days of the planet.

Her sensors showed no sign of *Skoll* and Marlena felt a sense of worry building in her chest. She knew Alex was the most capable pilot she had ever flown with, probably even better than she was, but she still worried for her son. If he didn't come through a slipstream soon, she had to trust he had a good reason for it.

Setting her auto-pilot toward home, she walked carefully back down to her quarters to be with her wounded son.

ABOUT THE AUTHOR

 Born on a snowy morning in LaGrande, Oregon, Joseph Mackay was raised with two brothers in Placerville, California. A born adventurer, Joseph has lived in an RV full time and off the back of a motorcycle, has flown a helicopter and enjoyed skydiving. When not writing, he enjoys playing bass guitar, weight lifting, playing with his dog "Mimi," watching Giants baseball, and preparing for his next adventure.

Interested in contacting me?
Please direct all emails to josephmackay@gmail.com

Want to stay current with the latest news and releases?
Check out: www.josephmackaybooks.com